Bradd Chambers

*in*

*too*

*deep*

Bradd Chambers

In Too Deep
Copyright © Bradd Chambers 2019
Published in 2019 by Kindle Direct Publishing,
Amazon

Bradd Chambers

Other publications from Bradd Chambers:

*'Someone Else's Life'*
Released June 2017
Available now on Amazon

*'Our Jilly'*
Released November 2017
Available now on Amazon

Bradd Chambers

*In Too Deep*

Bradd Chambers

For anyone who has ever lost
someone to the River Foyle.

Bradd Chambers

# Prologue:

I can't believe I'm actually doing this. The wind howls in my ears and whips my hair across my face. My hand battling to steady the strands and pull them back behind my ears. Pulling the hood over my head further. My scarf tied around my face, muffling my sobs. Blinking away tears, I stagger forward, embracing the cold sharp slaps of air hitting my exposed skin.

Leaving the vegetation in my wake, my right side is greeted by the grandeur of the houses shadowed by the bridge, the Gleneagles Estate leaking from the main Culmore Road. The houses I always dreamed of living in when I was little. I bet they're happy, the odd pungent scent of the river the only thing to disrupt their lives.

As I continue the incline, I'm surrounded on both sides by railings. Railings to my left stopping me from barrelling into oncoming traffic, something easily done in conditions like these. Railings on my right protecting me from a deadly fall into the infamous River Foyle. Not that they'll be much help when I climb over them.

You see, in this city especially, the river is a solution to the people's problems. An easy way out of a bad situation. Suicide rates are the highest in Northern Ireland than the rest of the UK, with around 300 every year. That's three times as many people as road accidents, and they've doubled within the past 20 years. Many of which are through drowning. In Derry, the vast majority from jumping the Foyle Bridge.

Is it too cliché to say I can feel my heart in my throat as I steal glances between the metal railings? Down into the bleak black water crashing along beneath me. People say they don't know how anyone could have the balls to do something like this. Some don't, of course. They come here for a cry for help, making sure someone's there to talk them down or hold their hand as they ship them off to Altnagelvin Hospital afterwards.

Whether they were ever going to jump or not relies solely within the person's frame of mind. You hear about it all the time. People saying that so-and-so would've been so scared they definitely would've had a heart attack before they hit the water. Or they would've changed their mind half way through and would've wanted to wade themselves back up in the air to land safely on their feet on the right side of the railings. But no one will ever know, will they? Will I?

I've reached the halfway point of the bridge now, where it's at its highest. Luckily, at this time of night, and with the weather, not many are brave enough to face the elements. Hopefully a lone taxi driver or night shift worker won't be here to stop me. Change my mind. Bring unwanted attention.

After all, I've said my goodbyes. It's just the way it has to be.

Gripping the freezing metal with both of my ungloved hands, the vertiginous drop is shielded momentarily as, once again, the south-easterly wind throws my hair into my face, obstructing my view. Rain water spitting at me from the Waterside of the city. Taking a deep breath and closing my eyes, I step forward to hoist myself up, memories of better times playing in my head to mask the pain.

Bradd Chambers

# Chapter One:

She almost trips over it in her rush to get through the door. Odd, she hadn't ordered anything online in a while. Swooping down and sliding it up her leg and torso until it's rested under her arm, she twists the key in the lock and topples into the house. Throwing it and her keys onto the hall table, she hobbles out of her heels and up the stairs.

It had been a hard day at work, politicians making her job even harder as they headlined the conference, and Mark had promised her a nice dinner in the city centre. Her stomach groans for some nice salmon from one of her favourite restaurants. It doesn't matter which one, they all seem to be owned by the same people if the rumours are true.

When she's had a whore's bath, changed into the sparkly dress and added some of the expensive perfume her mum used to wear, she rings the taxi. A 20 minute wait? Taxis are a joke in this town. Padding down the stairs and lifting her discarded heels, she boils the kettle whilst she fights herself back into them. Despite her feet being blistered and bruised from the long day cramped in them, she knows they're the only ones that match this dress.

Battle over, she exhales and lays back, sweat already glistening on her forehead. That's when she remembers the package. Filling her cup and leaving the teabag in for more strength, she grabs it and dumps herself on the sofa. Thoughts of a wrong delivery dispersed as she checks the name and address before tearing off the packaging.

It's a plain white box. Opening the lid, her mouth forms an *'o'* shape as she examines the designer shoes. Merlot red with a seven-inch stiletto heel wrapped in gold tissue paper with the designer brand etched onto it. It takes her a few moments, after gawping at the shoes, to notice the note. Unfolding it, it simply says:

*'Ava, I love you, M x.'*

A smile engulfs her face. It isn't even her birthday or anything. And these will go perfectly with this dress. She glides her feet into them. They're surprisingly comfortable as she struts up and down her hall, flourishing them in front of the long mirror. She has the most thoughtful boyfriend ever.

# Chapter Two:

Mark's by the bar checking his phone when she creeps up behind him, grabbing his waist and jerking him with a light '*boo.*' He turns and smiles at her, planting a kiss on her cheek.

"Alright, gorgeous?"

"Exhausted and starving, but happy," Ava smiles, scrunching her shoulders up in the cute way that sends Mark's heart racing.

She kicks her heel out slightly, rubbing his shin with it. Mark smirks from the corner of his mouth.

"That happy, eh?"

"Why wouldn't I be?"

"Bit of a public place, keep it until we get home," he blushes, pressing himself against her.

She sniggers and wraps an arm around him, resting her head on his chest. After everything she's been through, he's always been there. She doesn't know what she'd do without him.

The waiter comes down the stairs and signals to Mark to follow them. Mark nods at him with a wink and turns to Ava, holding his arm out for her to link onto him. That's when Ava realises.

The new shoes. The fancy restaurant. The cheeky wink to the waiter. This is it. He's going to propose.

As they climb the stairs to the seating area above, her heart beats aggressively through her chest. Of course, she'll say yes. But with everything in work and her being so much younger than him, would it be a good idea to get engaged right now? She always imagined being financially stable, living with her boyfriend and planning the wedding within nine or ten months. She never wanted a drawn-out engagement where the spark fizzles out and everyone contemplates whether you ever actually will get married.

But then again, Mark makes a good lot of cash. Just because all her money is tied up in her charity work, it doesn't mean that they couldn't organise a modest wedding with the little money they both have saved up. And Mark's parents wouldn't see them stuck. With Mark their only child, they've got loads in the bank. After all, they did pay for all his tuition fees through university, gave him a considerable amount to start up his own business and helped with the deposit on his house. And after a while, what's mine is yours and all that.

Ava gets a stab of guilt at thinking such a thing as Mark pulls back her chair for her, giving a dramatic impression of a butler that makes the little girl at the table beside them giggle. He smiles over at her as he takes his seat opposite Ava.

"Can I get you anything to drink?"

"Well, I wouldn't mind a bottle of bubbly. We're celebrating after all," his eyes light up as he wiggles his eyebrows at Ava, the butterflies in her stomach feeling like they're trying to escape up her throat and out of her mouth.

"I'll have a strawberry daquiri, please," Ava smiles sweetly at the waiter.

Does he know?

As he nods politely at them both, he skirts off down the stairs to the bar they just recently vacated, seen perfectly from the bannister beside them. Ava watches him meticulously. Craning her neck to see if he's adding anything to her champagne flute, then she sees Mark watching her and smiles. She doesn't think he'd be that corny anyway.

"What're you staring at?" she blushes.

"Just so lucky to have you," he turns his head to the side. "How was work?"

"Oh," she waves the topic away, "we don't have to talk about that."

"I want to."

He does. He always does. He shows such an interest in her life.

"Just the same old shit," her lips purse.

She picks up her daiquiri, smiling at the waiter as he brings out the expensive-looking bottle from the ice bucket and swerves its label in Mark's direction for approval. Not that it's any use anyway, the two glasses are already steaming with fizz. She doesn't like discussing work in company. He knows that. She gazes into her champagne glass. No ring? No problem. She returns her attention to Mark's face as the waiter leaves. The lines on his face are getting deeper. He's not even 30 yet.

"Politicians still against everything?" he puts down the menu he only examined for seconds.

"Oh, aye. The norm. Saying we're doing a good thing, but our interests are in the wrong place. The money will be better spent increasing the height of the railings or having a net. They're too blind to see that that isn't the solution to the problem."

She realises her voice is getting more and more raised and her hand hurts from gripping her drink tightly. She exhales and puts her glass down, tucking her hair behind her ears. He's heard all of this before. Hundreds of times. There's no use getting annoyed about it, especially in public. He's on her side. He grabs her hand from across the table and leans forward, their eyes meeting.

"She'd be so proud of you. You know that."

She smiles back tears and grips his hand tighter.

"Anyway," she coughs, reaching for her drink. "What are we celebrating?" she raises her eyebrows and her glass.

"Well, I was going to wait until after dinner because it's a long sort of story that I didn't want to coincide with the delicious food for my starving other half," he winks.

She laughs nervously. What's he getting at? This isn't making sense. She lowers her glass with a puzzled look.

"I've just bought the place on Carlisle Road."

Her mouth falls open and she half nods. Oh, this is what it was? The business he's been itching to get at for a few weeks now. How could she have been so stupid? He cocks his head to the side in confusion before she jerks into action.

"Oh, oh. Babe, well done. That's great. I'm so happy for you."

She raises her glass and clinks it against his, downing the champagne in one whilst he continues to give her a muddled look. Wiping her mouth with her napkin, she goes to stand.

"Ava..."

"I'm just nipping to the loo. If the waiter comes, tell him I want the salmon. And a side salad. And fill my glass for me," she laughs too loudly, pointing at her empty flute.

Turning, she jostles clumsily past waiters taking orders and customers sidestepping one another to get back to their seats. She hides her face from the tables as she descends the stairs, rushing to get to the toilets before the tears come.

# Chapter Three:

He stands as he looks up to her returning.

"Ava, what's wrong?"

She waves away his concerns as she sits down and pulls her chair in tight against the table.

"Nothing, nothing. It's stupid."

"It isn't stupid. Please, talk to me."

She looks at him from across her glass, drinking as much as she can before the silence becomes awkward. She burps silently as she puts down her drink. She only had half a sandwich for lunch and nothing else but a few cups of tea all day. The bubbles are starting to go to her head.

"It's seriously nothing. I didn't sleep well last night worrying about the meeting. Then it went atrocious as expected. Then I was rushing to get home to get here and there was the new shoes you got me and the champagne and the celebrations and the confusion and I was just being stupid. I thought..." She wrinkles her nose.

"You thought I was going to ask you to move in with me?"

Ava blinks stupidly.

"Aye, aye... That's it."

"Ave, we've had this discussion before. You said you're perfectly happy on your own."

"And I am. I'm just being oversensitive, ignore me. I'm being stupid. Just stupid..." She laughs, covering her eyes with her hands.

"Nothing about you is stupid," Mark wraps his hand around her arm, pulling her hand away softly. "I'm sorry if I made you feel like that. I promise it wasn't intentional."

Ava smiles back, feeling a little better. She shakes her head and goes back to her daiquiri. She was jumping to conclusions. It had been a hard day. She should just relax and enjoy the meal.

After the waiter takes their orders, she listens attentively to Mark's story about how he jostled with the business owner on Carlisle Road. How he had told Mark the hairdressers would never be able to pass as an accountants. There was too much work to be done. Mark even managed to haggle the price down by £1,500 because he explained to the owner how much he had in place already. Who he knew and who he was already speaking to about the renovations.

It makes Ava forget about her earlier outburst completely. Until, half way through their starter of chicken wings, Mark sits up straight and looks at her, a slither of sauce drooling down his chin.

"What?" she giggles.

"What did you say earlier about new shoes?"

"These?" Ava struggles a leg out from under the table and kicks a heel in the air for him to see.

"When did you get them?"

Tucking her leg back in, Ava blinks at him.

"Today. You got me them?"

"I did?" Mark laughs.

"Yeah?"

"Erm... No, I didn't."

"They were waiting at my front door when I got back from work. They had a note in the box saying *'love you'* and signed *'M.'"*

Mark wipes his chin whilst shaking his head.

"That wasn't me."

Ava drops her half-eaten chicken wing and squints at him.

"It has to be you."

"It wasn't, babe. I swear. What would I know about shoes?"

Ava nods. It's true. They've been together three years now and every birthday, Christmas or anniversary he'd always present her with jewellery. His aunt works in a jewellers and although neither of them mention it, it's an unspoken agreement that it's her that tells him what to buy.

"Definitely *'M?'"*

"Definitely."

"You wouldn't have read the writing wrong?"

"It was printed."

Another hint that made her believe it was Mark, his handwriting is awful. The cards he gets her are special prints from Moonpig or some similar site.

"Who else do you think it could be?"

Ava goes through her contacts in her head. Matthew? Melissa? Mikayla? No, none of them would ever buy her a present, let alone tell her they love her.

"What about your man in work?"

"Who?"

"The one you headlined the conference with today?"

Lightbulb.

"Michael?"

"Aye, him."

She turns her nose up at the thought.

"He's an ol' man."

"And? Pretty girl like you should be fighting them off with a shitty stick."

She laughs and continues eating.

"But the *'I love you'* part?"

"Did it definitely say '*I love you*?'"

Ava stares at the painting behind Mark, wracking her brain to remember.

"I'm sure it did."

"Would it have said, *'Love, M?'*"

She shrugs.

"But that's still weird."

"You've always said he's very overly friendly."

"Yeah, but towards everyone. It's just his personality. I don't think he has a special interest in me. And he knows I have a boy- ... Have you."

"Snake," he winks.

They laugh.

"Maybe he bought them for your conference? Wanted you to look your best?"

"I can buy my own shoes, I don't need his help," she frowns. "But if he did, then he would've asked why I wasn't wearing them this morning?"

"Maybe he was too embarrassed? In case you didn't like them or something?"

"Maybe..." Ava purses her lips as the waitress picks up their plates filled with chicken carcasses.

She can't imagine him doing such a thing. He's never been anything other than professional. And she has the strong impression he's gay. But the thought of a co-worker wanting her to look her best for an important conference makes her feel better other than the looming feeling that had come over her head once Mark had denied all involvement.

"...Maybe..."

# Chapter Four:

Landing home to the sight of Robyn's car in Ava's driveway makes Mark give her a look of contempt. It's going to be a long night. Parking on the pavement, Ava sighs as she steps out of the passenger side of the car. All the attention is going to be on Robyn now, and all she's itching to do is check that note.

Stepping into her hallway, she hears the calls of Robyn from the sitting room. Painting a smile on, she throws her jacket onto the seat and gazes over at Robyn on the sofa, her feet on the pouffe with the TV on. You'd swear she lives here.

"Well, what have you two love birds been up to?" Robyn winks at Mark as he pops his head around the door.

"Just out for dinner," he smiles back, before retreating and giving Ava a face that makes her know he's in no mood to deal with Robyn tonight.

Coughing slightly and taking a seat beside her, Ava looks deep into Robyn's eyes.

"Rob, what have I told you about that spare key? It's for emergencies only."

"Oh, I know. I do know, Ava. But I just couldn't be cooped up in that house any longer.

Since Damien left, I've just been so lonely. You understand that, don't you?"

Ava stares at the TV and sighs as discreetly as she can. Always the guilt trip with Robyn. The golden paper catches her eyes as she gazes over at where she discarded the box, just beside the fireplace.

"I know, Robyn. But I've had a long day at work. And I'm with Mark. We've just came back from a date night."

Robyn does an overexaggerated gasp, her hand pressed against her chest and her eyes wide, as if she had no idea.

"How silly of me. I should've known you'd be with Mark. Where is he now?"

Ava blinks repeatedly and stares at her aunt. Surely she can't be getting that bad?

"You just saw him. Just now. At the door," she turns and points at her living room door.

Turning back to Robyn, she watches her nod and smile in the way she does when Ava knows she has no idea what's going on.

"Right you be, I'll leave you sure. Don't need some gooseberry ruining things for you."

She stumbles to her feet, Ava also standing with relief. Usually it's not this easy. Robyn coughs as she picks up her handbag, but Ava still hears it. The clinking noise.

"What was that?" she narrows her eyes.

"What was what?" Robyn puckers her lip in delusion.

"Let me see your bag," Ava extends her hands.

Robyn rolls her eyes and hands it over. Unzipping the handbag, Ava roots around through the cigarettes, perfume and money until she finds what she's looking for. Mini bottles of wine.

"Rob. You know you're not supposed to drink with the tablets you're on. The doctor said-"

Robyn waves away her nagging.

"The doctors don't know shit. I'm grand," she gazes into Ava's eyes, as if trying to hypnotise her.

Ava stares back, looking her aunt up and down. She doesn't seem as bad as she normally is when she does drink. So, putting down the two full bottles and giving Robyn the bag back, the other two empties tucked under her arm, she escorts her out to the car. She might've had a few glasses of bubbly and half a daiquiri, but she's in a far better state to drive than Robyn is.

# Chapter Five:

When Ava has Robyn safely in her own house, she apologises before leaving and driving the ten-minute journey back. Thankful that she meets no police on the way home, she groans as she pulls in behind Mark's car. Robyn's been hard work this past year. After everything that's happened, she was so helpful and there for Ava, which makes her feel even more guilty for feeling annoyed with her.

Doctors still don't know what's wrong. They thought maybe it was the early signs of dementia, but there isn't enough evidence for a diagnosis. And it's almost as if she picks and chooses her moods and when she doesn't remember things. Mark thinks it's the trauma. The drink doesn't help. Since everything that happened, she's been drinking a lot and on loads of different medications to help with her anxiety and sleeping. She only stopped shaking a year after it happened, ten failed prescriptions later. People seem to think that because she was so strong for Ava that she took a backseat to her own emotions, and they finally caught up with her.

The brain's an odd thing, Ava thinks, as she climbs her drive. Her bedroom curtains are closed, meaning Mark's already gone to bed. She checks her watch, it's only gone 10pm. Mark's been so patient with her and her family's issues, but sometimes he just can't take a lot of it.

After taking a few moments to tidy up after Robyn, she climbs the stairs to see Mark in bed, his back to the door. Slipping into her shorts and an old t-shirt, she climbs in beside him and wraps an arm around him.

"You awake?"

He moans sleepily.

"I'll leave you to sleep," she goes to pull away, but he holds her hand tightly.

"No, I want to see you," he turns and smiles at her, his eyes still full of dreams. "Did you get her home okay?"

"Aye, sorry about her. Just having one of her episodes."

"There's no reason to apologise. It's me that should be. I've had a long day and just wanted to come back and crawl into bed with you."

She smiles as he slides his hands under her top and up her front. He leans in to kiss her lips and she lets go of all the stress of the day as he migrates down to her neck.

# Chapter Six:

Lying afterwards on her damp sheets, Ava allows herself to relax as she rests her head on his chest. Feeling his heartbeat slow down to normal, and his breathing get deeper and longer until the hint of a snore is audible. She smiles and pulls in closer beside him. He grumbles incomprehensibly as she gives way to sleep.

She finds herself at the front of a long table in a conference room, lined with suits and scowled expressions. At the head of the table sits Darrell Boyle, the politician from this afternoon's meeting. He's standing with one hand on the table and the other pointing accusatorily towards her.

"Why do you care? It's all your fault anyway," he bellows, spit flying from his mouth.

The suits nod in unison before their featureless faces blur with the oncoming of her tears. She blinks them away and turns towards the door, but it's not there. She follows the walls around four corners, palms pressed flat against them. But it's no use. There isn't one. She's trapped. All the while, they shout abuse and hurl scrunched up balls of paper at her.

"It's all your fault."

"She never loved you."

"Kill yourself!"

She shakes her head, sliding down the wall until she's on the ground, pressing her hands against her ears and wrapping her elbows around her knees, willing for them to stop.

"Ava?"

Through the chaos, she opens one eye and looks up. There stands Michael, the shoebox thrust in her face, a wide grin on his face.

"What do you think, Ava? Nice, aren't they? I picked them myself," he purses his lips in the smug, camp way he presents new information to her.

"What do you want?" she hisses, the chants getting louder and louder as the crowd circles Michael and get closer and closer, their mind-numbing faces inches from her own.

"What do you want?" Ava screams.

Then, she's awake. She bolts upright, fresh sweat on her body and sheets. Mark grunts and rolls on his side, sliding the duvet off her. She slaps her hands to her head, forcing herself to calm down until the shadows engulfing her room return to normal from their hypersensitive, demonic form. She has to know.

Gazing at Mark for a few more moments, his snores building, she knows he's in a heavy sleep. Picking up her clothes from the foot of the bed, she struggles into them, sticking to her sweaty body as soon as she pulls them on. She pads down the stairs, thankful for the concrete below the carpet, for wood would give her mission away.

Reaching the living room, she turns on the tiny lamp and gets down on her knees on the rug to pull the shoebox towards her. Her hands trembling as she pushes the tissue paper out of the way to find the note.

*'Ava, I love you, M x.'*

She knew it. She knew it said *'I love you.'*

Dropping her hands from her face, she shakes her head and stares into the corner. Who would send this? Could it be Michael? She doubts it, but she'll see him in the office tomorrow, so she can slyly bring it up then. She doesn't want too much attention brought to it. She'll mention to Mark tomorrow to not tell anyone else either.

A shadow crossing the window makes her jump. She falls back onto her bum, her hand flying out to steady the landing. She gazes out of the massive window which takes up the majority of the wall. Out onto her lawn, the lonely tree swaying in the wind, and the desolate street. Her neighbour's houses darkened apart from the one solitary light she knows Mrs McVeigh uses in her hall to help her guide her way to the toilet in the middle of the night.

It could've been a flicker of her imagination, or a bat or bird flying past the streetlamp, temporarily blocking the light shining into her window. Nonetheless, she struggles to her feet, hastily draws her curtains and stands with her back to them. Too petrified to make the two-step journey from her living room door to the stairs, leaving herself fully vulnerable to the front door and the windows either side.

*In Too Deep*

Bradd Chambers

\*\*\*\*

I remember the first time I met Chris. I was forced into a work night out, closing the shop that night and taken by surprise. At ten minutes to six, the remaining staff that weren't working strutted into the shop.

"It's your birthday, we're obviously heading out," Rachel had hugged Christina.

I pursed my lips, a bit annoyed that Christina had joined the troops up the stairs to finish getting ready, leaving me alone on the shop floor. Luckily, Phil joined me.

"It's the girl's birthday, we can spare her for a few minutes to get her face on," he cackled, clinging onto my arm.

I always had a soft spot for Phil. Ever since the day I'd interviewed him. I'd been really strict and cold with my colleagues as I'd travelled up the career ladder. But he brought something out in me. Something that made me forget about the shy little girl that I once was. I just clicked with him instantly. We got each other. He got on with everyone else as well, ultimately making me form relationships more with the other staff.

As soon as I put down the shutter, I climbed the stairs with the till drawer, bypassing the gaggle of girls gathered around the lonely mirror in the hall. After I banked the money in the safe, I was looking forward to getting home. Even thought about swinging by Robyn and Damien's for a takeaway. But I was also annoyed that they'd all left without even saying goodbye.

A juvenile thought, I knew, but I couldn't help it. My other friends had pissed off to London and the likes. I was the only one in my group to remain in Derry. The troubles driving people away. The clothes shop was struggling as it was, despite being in the middle of the city centre. But when I exited the office, all the girls were still there.

"Oh, alright guys? Just gonna close up now if you are nearly done?"

Phil put his arms around me.

"We're waiting for you, Fee."

I was shocked.

"Me?"

"Aye, we're going to the bar. C'mon with us."

"Awk, I haven't been out in the town in years."

"Even more reason to head out then," Phil sang as he basically dragged me down the stairs.

*In Too Deep*

Bradd Chambers

# Chapter Seven:

She sits in the carpark, people watching, to give herself time to collect her thoughts. Almost everyone that parks here are either doing so to run the small stretch of Spencer Road to their places of work, or going to the new Waterside Health Centre on the same street, the giant windows giving the patients a beautiful vista of the River Foyle and the city embanking it.

She'd finally found the strength and courage to belt it up the stairs after a half hour of battling with herself last night. What followed was a very sleepless night, with Mark snoring beside her. Not that that's what was keeping her awake. Every creak of the house, passing car or rustling of leaves made her ears strain for signs of life. She must've drifted into a fitful slumber after five o'clock, but the alarm came too quick and she feels like the less than two-hour snooze has made her feel worse rather than better.

Mark coiled when she suggested that he keep the mystery of the shoes a secret. Advocating in the signature grumpy manner he resides in until his third cup of coffee that maybe by failing to ask anyone that she was building it up too much in her head. She knows he is right. But who could it be?

Almost as if on cue, Michael pulls up in his Mercedes beside her. He smiles and waves, mouthing to her dramatically, asking if she's coming in. She raises two fingers and flaunts her phone in front of her. Nodding, she can hear the faint whistling as he turns at the bank, making the two-minute walk to the office cheerily on this sunny morning.

Sighing and giving herself a light pep-talk, she steps out of her car, locking it and following him in the shoes that she fell in love with at first sight, only for recent revelations to taint them. But she knows it's the only way he could willingly mention them to her.

# Chapter Eight:

The wind chimes jingle to announce her presence as she opens the door and crosses the threshold into the space they've rented for just over a year. Despite not having a lot of money when she set up the charity, the landlord seemed to recognise her from her appearances in the local rags and dropped the rent significantly. A rumour circulated from the tiny, five-man team that his nephew had committed suicide almost a decade earlier, so it seemed he had a soft spot for them. Not only that, but he let her design the space, sending in his own men and paying them himself.

He'd done a lot for the company, even letting his mate Michael know about the volunteering vacancies. Michael took early retirement from Foyle College in 2012 when half the staff were replaced by younger models. Despite this, he'd always been interested in mental health, and still argues today for school funding money to be spent on counselling services for the students, depicting that teenage years are hard going, and some people might need to talk. He'd got a special recognition at the leaver's ceremony, which had instantly made Ava sit up and take in his application.

Now, there he sits at the back of the office, one hand on the mouse of his computer and another holding a cup of coffee, the same huge grin on his face.

"Alright, Ave?"

"Aye, Michael. You?"

"Grand, grand," he nods his head towards the mug on her desk. "Milk and two sugars."

She blushes.

"Thank you, Michael."

"So," he raises his eyebrows and purses his lips as she sits down. "How was date night then?"

"Aye, it was nice."

"Where'd you go?"

"Quaywest."

"Hmmm, let me think... 50/50 with tobacco onions?"

"No, had the salmon actually."

"Ohhhh," Michael winks, "excuse us. Fancy pants paying, was he?"

She turns her head towards the computer and enters her password. She doesn't like when people talk about Mark's money. Although it may be in jest, she hates the fact of anyone thinking she's some sort of gold-digger.

"Looks like it's not the only thing he paid for," Kat, a fifty-year-old single mum at the desk behind Ava, squints. "What are those beauties?"

Ava follows her gaze down to her feet. To her shoes. Pushing her hair behind her ear, she instinctively looks at Michael, who nods with wide eyes.

"Erm... No, actually. Mark didn't buy me these."

"They look expensive," Kat lifts her mug and nods towards them again. "Much?"

I don't know, Ava thinks, willing Michael to inform her as much. She would 100% pay him back. When she doesn't answer, Michael stands and swerves between the desks towards the printer already bursting to life, supplying them with dozens of posters for their latest fundraiser on Wednesday.

"Nosy was hung," he wags his finger at Kat, who scowls back at him. "If Ava wants to treat herself every now and then, she can. Who else will?"

He rests a reassuring hand on her shoulder, a warm smile on his face. She surprises herself by grimacing and edging away from him. So it isn't him? Surely it's not his fault, and she shouldn't take it out on him. He senses her tension and holds two hands up, palms facing forward, before moving to the printer and inspecting the latest copy.

"These should be ready for Facebook and Twitter and that by this afternoon, Ava. What you think?" He holds the red poster towards her and she half-pretends to scan it.

"Looks great, Michael. Sorry, I'm just not myself today."

"Hope you're not pregnant," he raises his eyebrows and chortles.

"Hope not too," she gives an attempt at a laugh, but it comes out sloppy and forced. "No, I barely slept the other night worrying about yesterday's meeting, and then too much drink last night meant I didn't get the best of sleeps then either."

The two nod as Claire fights her way through the door, her arms filled with the typical handbag and shopping bags with Christ knows what in them. She'll never show up without half her house with her.

"I think I'm just going to step outside for some air," Ava coughs, but the others are too preoccupied in their own conversations to give her much attention.

She heads to the back area where there's a small meeting room and kitchen, before pushing the back door. Sitting on the step, she sighs and covers her head from the already blistering sun. Who could this be? Bringing out her phone, she scrolls through her list of people with names beginning with *'m.'* Another fruitless attempt, as no one would be overly close with her. She keeps her distance with people. Ever since...

A knock at the window in front brings her back to her senses. Looking up, she sees Michael with one hand to his head, his thumb and pinky finger extended with the other three curled in, his attempt to tell her that there's someone on the phone for her.

"Hello, Foundation for Fiona. Ava speaking. How can I help you?"

She's breathless as she reaches her phone.

"Hi, Ava. This is Cathal O'Flaherty from the Londonderry Letter. I'm just wondering if I could interview you regarding your conference yesterday to prohibit raising the railings on the Foyle Bridge?"

The boy sounds like he's reading straight from the press release. Ava rolls her eyes towards her colleagues to show that it isn't anything serious, and they return back to their screens, uninterested in anything that doesn't involve raising money or awareness.

# Chapter Nine:

It doesn't take Ava long to walk the short distance down Spencer Road to their destination. Whereas her charity, the FFF as they call it, is at one end of the road, closer to Clooney Terrace, the Londonderry Letter is at the other, closer to Victoria Road and the Craigavon Bridge into the town.

Their meeting point is the Sandwich Company, a little up the street from the paper's headquarters. She still gets there before the journalist, ordering herself a tea and a sandwich and taking a comfier looking chair towards the back of the café. Ten minutes later, she sees him crossing the road, pushing open the door and searching the room, nodding when she acknowledges him, before ordering a coffee from the barista.

As he waits for his drink, she inspects him discreetly. He's much younger than she expected. Wearing a wrinkled shirt far too big for him and bum fluff on his chin that can't be passed off as a five o'clock shadow. There's something oddly familiar about him, but she can't decide what. He catches her staring at him and she smiles, returning to her hot drink until he crosses the room.

"Ava?"

"Aye, nice to meet you," she hovers out of her chair as she takes his proffered hand.

He sits opposite her, bringing out his notepad from his back pocket.

"So, basically I want my story to have a bit of meat. The press release I received was just facts, facts, facts. I want emotion," his eyes light up as he speaks, his hands flailing around dramatically.

She can tell he's very passionate, whether about mental health in general or just his job is unknown, as he continues his spiel. So many people in this city are affected by suicide. It takes her a while before she realises that he must have asked her a question, as he stares at her in silence. She wracks her brain to remember what he was saying.

"I'm happy to help," she nods.

He smiles back. Good save.

"So..."

He licks the tip of his finger as he flicks through his overfilling notepad before resting on a blank page. Hovering the pen over the page, he glances up at her.

"Tell me, why don't you want the railings of the Foyle Bridge higher?"

Ava leans back, getting herself comfortable.

"It's not that I don't want the railings higher. Obviously, that would be great. But, in complete contrast to suicide, it's a temporary solution to a permanent problem."

She watches as he writes in shorthand, his hand flying across the page, his brow frowned slightly.

"There are... What? Dozens of ways to kill yourself? The Foyle Bridge is merely one of them. If we raise the railings, or put a net down, someone isn't going to decide against suicide. They'll just find another way, won't they?

"What we *really* need is more facilities and money being put into the mental health community. I understand there's doctors and counsellors and that, but, in the experience of some people that have came to us, that could take weeks, months. That's too long. Someone suffering with mental health issues, whether having suicidal thoughts or not, should have a place to go and chat. Obviously, we urge people to talk to loved ones, but some people aren't comfortable with that. Some prefer a complete stranger. Or a professional.

"There isn't enough money being put into the NHS for mental health. That's why I set up this charity. I want to provide the people with a solution. Train up counsellors, God knows there's plenty of them graduating from the colleges and universities every year. But they go off somewhere else. You know why? Because there's no jobs for them here.

"We need facilities in the town where anyone can go to talk things through, or get prescriptions if that's what they need. But they can't wait that long. The doctors' surgeries are so packed, if you want to go for the common cold, by the time you get an appointment, it's been and gone. You're cured. I respect Darrell Boyle and his party's offers, and the people of this town's pleas and petitions, I really do. But the money should be used elsewhere, for solutions rather than deterrents."

It takes a while for Cathal to stop writing, so Ava takes a sip from her tea, now gone lukewarm. After a few minutes, he looks up, smiling. Shifting in his seat, sticking a foot under his bum in a juvenile way, he gazes at her for several moments. Drinking her in. She stares back. Why is he so familiar?

"Do you think the extended railings, or nets, would be an eyesore?"

She protrudes her bottom lip and shakes her head.

"I don't know. Maybe? But that isn't the main issue he-"

"You lost your mother to suicide, right?"

"I did, aye."

She doesn't like where this is going.

"And how did she die, if you don't mind me asking?"

I do, she thinks.

"She entered the river."

"So, she jumped?"

"She did," she bites her tongue.

He wants to be sharp with her? She'll be the same back.

"Would you not, taking in your own experience, therefore, want to protect others from feeling the way you've felt for the past three years?"

"Yes, that's exactly why I'm doi-"

"And would that not be possible with there being no way to jump from the Foyle Bridge?"

"That would be great, in an ideal world, yes. But what's to stop them overdosing? Hanging themselves? Getting drunk and driving into a bloody wall? If a net or a higher railing or any of that other craic could stop suicide completely, then happy days. I'd be all for it. But, it's not that easy. You're not looking at the bigger picture here. We need to stop people feeling suicidal, not limit the ways in which they can take their own lives!"

She coughs and looks around her, flustered. A few people have stopped their conversations and are staring at her, embarrassingly looking away once she makes eye contact with them.

"It isn't your company's own money that they're spending on the railings, correct?"

"Correct, but think about how expensive that would be for the taxpayers. If we added our money together, who knows how many counsellors we could fund. Not everyone in this city has money to be throwing at big fancy therapists with their degree certificates on the wall and luxurious settees to lounge on. Sometimes, an ear to listen is all these people need.

"Which is what we're trying to do. To open a small space in the city centre where people can feel safe. Volunteers to start out, before gradually getting in professionals. We're planning a fundraiser on Wednesday. The details will be released within the next few hours. We want people to come support us. Help us raise the money and awareness we need for this space."

Cathal observes her for a moment longer, he hadn't written any of what she had just said down. Finally, when the silence gets unbearable, he sits forward.

"Are you aware of the suicide prevention programme in place in San Francisco, Ava?"

Ava gives a nervous laugh.

"Yeah, I am fully aw-"

"The Golden Gate Bridge is just over 80-years-old," he ignores her. "Yet, there has been close to 2,000 deaths from people jumping off. That we know of," he raises an eyebrow. "They've put in a programme to place nets around it. It's taking years. But, with that in place, that will save who knows how many lives in the future."

"You don't know that," Ava spits. "And America is very different to Derry. I'm sure there's lots of money to throw about in San Francisco, on both mental health and physical preventions. But, in case you haven't noticed, we aren't very prosperous here, are we, Cathal? You're a reporter, I'm sure you know of all the budget cuts, closing down shops and God knows what else? We need all the money that we can get, and that's what I'm here for. I want to raise awareness, collect money and put it to good use, with or without Boyle's help."

A smirk is prominent on Cathal's face. Draining his untouched coffee in one, he stands and thanks Ava for her time before she watches him skirt around the dispersed chairs and tables and step out onto the street, losing him as he leaves the glass of the shop window behind. Ava stares after him in disbelief. How could that have gone any worse?

# Chapter Ten:

It wasn't posted. The parcel. It was hand delivered. After coming home from work an hour early, Ava sat again on her rug, examining the parcel over and over for some sort of clue as to who could've sent it. Then, she remembered the novel she read last summer on holidays, where a crazy ex-husband was able to track down his wife through the stamps on the letter she wrote him. Ava checked the front of the parcel, but there was no sign of any postage whatsoever. Just her name and her address in bold capital print.

That means, whoever sent her this, hadn't sent it at all. They dropped this on her front doorstep. The thought sends a shiver down her spine. Someone had crossed her beautifully kept lawn. Had stood in front of her front door. Possibly looked in through her windows at the life she made. Did they try and get in? Thank God she is religious on locking the doors and windows.

Should she contact the police? Surely they have enough on their plate without chasing up something as silly as this? She's sure the money that would be spent on fingerprint analysis would be worthwhile if there was some threat of violence in the package. Or a weapon of some sorts. But shoes? Gorgeous shoes? She can't imagine the police wasting their time.

Should she go around the neighbours and ask if they seen anything? Anything, or anyone, out of the ordinary? But how could she do that without arousing suspicion? A thousand thoughts run through her head. Thinking and thinking of ways for a legitimate reason to ask around. None spring to mind.

Maybe she could talk to Dermott? He's retired now, but he'd been so helpful when he was in the police force. She thinks back to the ways he helped her. A broken and alone 17-year-old. But the thought of talking about it out loud to anyone scares her.

It's hard enough discussing it with Mark. She'd texted him just after lunch to ask if he'd kept it a secret. She'd gotten a curt confirmation in reply. Maybe she is just making this all up in her head? Making a big deal out of nothing? But she can't help it, she's programmed like this. To think the worst. Ever since that night.

Bradd Chambers

\*\*\*\*

So, there I was. Out the town. For the first time in years. And you know what? I was actually enjoying myself. After a few vodkas, I'd let my hair down. Literally and metaphorically. I was chatting away, even surprising myself, and everyone else, with giving Christina a birthday hug. But it was half way through the night. When Phil had actually managed to get me drunk enough to loosen me up on the dancefloor. That's when I saw him.

We were bopping along to Whigfield's '*Saturday Night*' and laughing at Rachel's ridiculous dance moves. I felt two hands on my hips as I jumped away from them. Turning around to square up to the culprit. I fell in love with him right away. His long blonde hair. His piercing green eyes. His wide smile. He held both hands up and shouted something that I couldn't hear.

"What?" I screwed up one eye, brandishing my hand to my ear in an attempt to hear him.

He leaned in close and I smelt his aftershave.

"Sorry, was only trying to squeeze past."

I smiled as I pulled away, winking at him and turning back to Phil. What was I at? Winking? Flirting? That wasn't me.

Phil told me much later on that his face dropped then. When he saw me dancing with him. Completely unaware of Phil's raging homosexuality.

Danielle pointed towards the toilet and I took her hand, deciding to join her.

"So, looks like you've pulled," Danielle giggled at me through the cubicle wall.

"Eh?" I laughed, zipping myself up and flushing the toilet.

"That boy with the blonde hair. He's been staring at you for ages. He must like you."

I guffawed as I washed my hands, her eyeing me suspiciously when she joined me.

"What's wrong? Got someone at home waiting for you?"

Definitely not, I felt like saying, but made do with shaking my head.

"Then go for it. He's gorgeous," she elongated the final word, rolling her eyes back in her head and laughing.

We staggered out of the toilets then, me trying to discreetly search the room for him. I found him by the bar. Grabbing Danielle's hand again, I marched us over. Where had this sudden confidence come out of? It must've been the vodka. I stepped into the throng of people at a spot far enough away that we didn't look keen, but close enough that he could see us. I felt his eyes on me and looked over quick enough to only flash him a swift smile.

"I'll get these," he handed the money over when we'd received our drinks and were faking to look in our bags for our cash.

"Thanks," Danielle raised her glass to him with a giggle, before deserting me.

Raising the straw to my lips, I took a sip while he ordered his pint. He tried to talk to me again, but I still struggled to hear him, my ears not adjusted to the loud music of the club. After the third attempt, and the arrival of his drink, he entwined our fingers together and dragged me along outside.

Bradd Chambers

# Chapter Eleven:

The alarm blares from her bedside cabinet. It needn't have bothered. She didn't sleep a wink anyway. Hoisting herself out of bed, her body too sore for a mere 20-year-old, she pads off to the shower.

What a night. She had given Mark a cheery text asking to stay over last night, not wanting to admit that she was too afraid to stay by herself. What would he think of her then? He hadn't replied until gone 10pm, stating he'd just got home from the new space and was to be up early in the morning to meet contractors. She let on that nothing was wrong. She couldn't lose him. She'd rather lose herself.

Last night was an uneasy one. She expected Robyn to come and collect her car, but there was no sign of her. Ava guessed she was still lying in her house pissed, and thought against contacting her. Instead, she dug out a frozen pizza she forgot she had from the very bottom of the freezer, under some meat-free chicken and fish she'd bought when she tried, and failed, to be a veggie not that long ago. Firing it in the oven, she manoeuvred herself around the house out of sight of windows.

Scaling along walls and dodging behind coat hangers and chairs. Anything to keep herself safe. Keep her hidden.

Of course, when darkness came, it made everything worse. She still has to put blinds up in the kitchen, and she cursed herself for her carelessness as she crept into the dark room on her hands and knees, the only light emanating from the oven. Crawling forward, she checked and double checked the two windows either side of her before her arm swung up to turn the oven off. Scalding her hand on the oven tray, the heatproof gloves too high for her reach, she escorted the pizza to the living room, deeming the confined place her only safe haven with the protection of the thick, blackout curtains.

Even there, the muted TV was the only source of light. So it's no surprise that cheese and tomato sauce cover the blanket and rug, as she looks down at the scene now in the light of day. Shaking her head, she picks up her purse and escapes from the front door, locking it maladroitly behind her. Although it can't be more than five metres to her car, it seems like it takes a year. She jumps with fright as Mrs McVeigh sings over to her, waving as she makes her daily commute to the shops down at Whitehouse. She smiles back and gives a lethargic wave, before she speeds off down the Buncrana Road.

She gazes out at everyone going about their daily lives. Commuting to work, taking the dog a walk or going a jog themselves. Who could *'M'* be? She feels like she's in one of those stupid teen TV shows based in the states. After everything that's happened, she vowed she would never live her life in fear, she made sure of that. But now?

# Chapter Twelve:

Pulling onto the Foyle Bridge to migrate to the Waterside of the city, where her business rests, she desperately tries and fails to stop herself from taking quick glances at the railings, just like she does every day. She follows the incline up before it settles out, looking at the rows of traffic in front of her accumulating at the Caw Roundabout, whether travelling deeper into the Waterside or going further afield left to Limavady or Coleraine, or even Belfast straight in front.

She comes to a stop behind a jeep, but is still on the bridge. Usually traffic isn't this bad. She would be much closer to the roundabout at this time of the morning. She cranes her neck to see past the beast of a vehicle, but gives up and turns the radio on, tapping her fingers incessantly on the wheel.

Not being able to drag herself away from the inevitable, she glares at the railings that were so important in her meeting the other day and the interview yesterday. There she's sat, on top of the suicide hotspot of Derry City. The murderer of her mother. Would it be so wrong to have them higher? After all, it *is* very easy to lift yourself over them. She gets flashbacks of Rose on the *Titanic*, dangling over the edge. Then her mother comes into her head. Like she always does. But no matter how many times she tries to shake the image away, it's there. Her mother gazing down into the unstoppable River Foyle.

How did her life become that bad? Ava tried to be a good daughter. She was a teenager, of course she was going to rebel. But a few puffs of a cigarette at the Nerve Centre that one time and a couple of weekends in Brooke Park with a two-litre bottle of cider couldn't have sent her mother over the edge. Could it?

The traffic moves at a slow pace. Stop and go. Stop and go. Crawling forward slightly using her clutch, despite having nowhere to go, and having to roll back again. She becomes impatient. Finally, there's a curve in the road and the jeep no longer obstructs the view. Her heart leaps as she sees the blue beacons. The flashing lights.

She's unwillingly taken back to that night. Arriving home late from sneaking out to an empty house. Being confused, she returned to her bed and fell into a happy sleep, smile on her face. Only to be woken hours later to a thunder of fists on her front door. Robyn ushering her out. Telling her everything was going to be okay. Police officers nodding to her and asking her questions in stifling hot rooms with nothing spare of a table with chairs and a camera with a blinking red light failing to disguise itself in the corner. The night her life changed. Forever.

# Chapter Thirteen:

"Sorry I'm late."

Ava blushes, jostling herself into the office. It's her business, for God's sake. If she can't show up on time, what example does that set the other volunteers?

"No sweat, pet," Michael doesn't take his eyes off his screen. "Was it the accident?"

"Yeah," she exhales, dropping her bags and kicking them under the desk.

"Bad?"

"Not sure, I never saw any casualties."

"Did you get a good gander?"

"Well, I was stuck on the new bridge for a half hour. Single lane traffic is always a nightmare. The cars looked smashed up, but the ambulances didn't leave, and I didn't see anyone that particularly beat up. Hopefully everyone's okay."

Michael nods along, still scrolling with his mouse, eyes sliding from one side of the screen to the other. Ava flops herself down in the swivel chair and turns to the back of the room. Claire and Paddy are discussing the looming weekend in the kitchen, fixing themselves drinks, but Kat's nowhere to be seen.

"At least I'm not the only one who has been stuck in the traffic," she says, turning to her computer and booting it up.

"Oh, Kat's phoned in sick, I'm afraid."

Ava curses herself.

"Looks like I *was* then," she gives a dry chuckle.

"Well, you're the only one to come from the city side now," Michael smiles over at her.

"Sorry."

"Don't apologise, it's hardly your fault."

Ava nods whilst she looks at the loading screen. Although this is, essentially, *her* business, she still finds it weird that these people who work for her can be two, sometimes three, times her age. It's took some adjusting, but so has everything in her life so far.

"Hi, Ava," Claire sings as she marches into the room, cup sloshing coffee onto the floor.

"Hiya," she gives a faint smile as she swivels around to greet her, before her eyes fix on the paper in Paddy's hand.

"Is that The Letter?"

She tries to hide the tremor in her voice. Afraid of what concoction Cathal has brewed up, another drama to spill onto her lap.

"It is," he hands it over.

Unfolding it on her desk, she sees a picture of herself, taken from the press release, on the bottom right hand side of the front page.

*'Extending the railings of the Foyle Bridge is a temporary solution to a permanent problem'* – *Ava McFeely. Full story page 6.'*

"You did well, Ave. Proud of you," Paddy gives a gummy smile.

Confused, Ava flicks through the first few pages of the newspaper, talking about business closures and sectarian attacks in the city, to find a huge picture of her mother on page 6.

*'Three years after the tragic death of Fiona McFeely, her daughter strives to increase awareness for mental health in the town.*

*'Ava McFeely was only a teenager when her mother entered the River Foyle, but since then she has devoted her life to making Derry City a happier place. Her efforts have included setting up a charity in her mother's name, Foundation for Fiona, and taking on the likes of Darrell Boyle, Health Minister for nationalist party...'*

Ava reads on, in complete shock that Cathal not only took her side, despite initially challenging her, but also could quote what she had said when he wasn't even taking notes.

"How's the comments on social media looking?" she asks the room after her third re-read.

"All positive," Claire beams from over her screen. "A lot of people are agreeing with you."

Tapping and double tapping the internet icon, impatient to see for herself, Ava has butterflies as her first impulse is to check Twitter.

*'@charles8kelly here here. Thank god someone's speaking sense.'*

*'@lornamichaela56 this brought a tear 2 my eye. I remember waking up to this news. So sad but proud of Ava for doing somefing with her life.'*

Ava's eyes brim with tears. Of course, there's the same old trolls, spurting out statistics and figures, or cursing her, but she ignores them. She learned to long ago.

"Right," she smacks her hands, a new lease of life that she didn't have ten minutes ago. "Wednesday is our absolute focus now. All hands on deck. He mentioned the evening at the end of the piece, so we get it out on all platforms right now. Michael, you're in charge of that," she points in his direction.

He nods and waves his hands.

"Your wish is my command, mistress."

"Claire, I want you to ring around youth clubs, crèches, anything with children or young people. See if you can forward the PDF onto them for them to print out for their notice boards. Kat-"

She stops herself.

"Er... Sorry. Claire, see if we can get any local celebrities, The girl off *The Apprentice*. Your man who was on *Big Brother*. If they can make an appearance, we can bet their fans will be there."

Claire salutes and turns to her computer promptly.

"Paddy-"

"One step ahead of you," he waves about the posters in his hand, slipping on his jacket with the other.

"Pubs, chippies, shops, bloody lampposts if you can," Ava smiles at him as he clicks his stapler in confirmation.

Ava sinks into her chair, smiling at the picture of her mum gazing up at her from the newspaper, the room around her bursting to life with sounds of telephone voices and the padding of keyboards. It was her favourite photo of her mum. Ava had taken it herself. In the living room before her mum had gone out for her Christmas do in work. Returning to her computer, she sees she's received a few more mentions. Scrolling through the hearty comments from strangers, she narrows her eyes at the recently updated notification.

*'@cathaloflahertylderryletter followed you.'*

# Chapter Fourteen:

Why is she nervous? She has no reason to be. She taps her foot zealously against the wooden frame of the bar before the bartender gives her an irritated smile, too polite to ask her to stop. She sucks on the straw of her cocktail, collecting the icy remnants by manoeuvring it around the glass, before ordering another, ignoring the brain freeze.

"Ava?"

She turns and smiles as Cathal drops his laptop bag on the floor, holding his hand out. She takes it with both her hands and eagerly shakes it.

"Thanks for agreeing to meet me."

"Of course, no problem," Cathal coughs, looking a lot more awkward in a bar scene, where he isn't in control of how the conversation is going to go.

"For your friend?"

The bartender perks his head towards Cathal.

"Er... I'll have a pint, please."

The two glance at each other uneasily while they wait for their drinks.

"Want to find a table?" Ava addresses the room in general rather than Cathal once they've arrived.

"Aye, alright."

They find a quiet corner of the room, beside the toilets. They'd agreed to meet in a bar at the very corner of Dungiven Road, where it meets the crossroads. Somewhere close to both of their offices. They sit and sip their drinks, smiling at each other awkwardly.

"I just…" Ava starts.

Cathal sits forward eagerly, his bottom lip covering his top.

"I just wanted to thank you," she blushes, focusing her eyes on her drink. "After the way we left things yesterday, I thought you were going to tear me apart for being a selfish bitch."

"Why would I do that?" he laughs, visibly getting a little more comfortable in his chair, the bubbles from the pint taking their effect.

"So many people think it," she narrows her eyes in case tears start to swell. "It's hard to ignore it sometimes. You know that saying, if someone calls you something often enough?" she smiles nervously, looking up to him observing her.

"I think what you're doing is very brave. I have massive respect for you."

"Then why the hassle? Why bring up San Francisco and such?"

For the first time, his eyes avert.

"To be honest, my editor told me to. Obviously, as a newspaper, we have to be impartial. And going up against Darrell Boyle? We can't do that unless we want ourselves in the firing line. You have some balls. I mean, don't get me wrong, he had me on the phone today instructing me to interview him too first thing Monday morning. But, I feel your pain. I see how passionate you are, and rightly so. These politicians, they never have experienced half as much pain as you have. They've lived a sheltered life. Breezed their way into a position of power and act like they can speak for us."

Ava nods along.

"That's exactly what I'm saying. Boyle probably has never had relations with anyone who has had suicidal thoughts. Mental illness has a stigma, everyone wants to brush it under the carpet because you can't physically see it. It's not fair."

Cathal nods and barrels into a new rant as Ava stares at him approvingly. Maybe she's made a new ally after all?

# Chapter Fifteen:

The pair talk for a while longer about politics, mental illness and the woes of the city. Three drinks later, and without any dinner or sleep, Ava's surprised to find herself slurring her words.

"Can I ask you a question?" Ava cocks her head to the side, deciding that Dutch courage will settle this once and for all.

"Aye, of course."

"I'm sorry, but you're just so familiar. I don't understand where I know you from?"

It had been plaguing Ava for the better part of an hour. She would remember his face if he came in looking for help and guidance, and through the chat he'd made no remarks about dealing with mental health issues himself. It couldn't be school, as she'd attended Thornhill, one of the Catholic all girl schools outside the city. That left friends' younger brothers, but she couldn't place an O'Flaherty she knew.

Cathal smirks.

"I interviewed you yesterday, remember?"

They laugh.

"No, seriously."

Cathal gazes at her a while longer.

"I must admit, I did feel the same when I saw you yesterday. It had annoyed me, but I remembered late last night. I used to hang out at the park a few years back. Drinking with my friends. We used to ask your mate, what was his name? Fuzzy? Fizzy?"

"Fizzbee!" Ava didn't mean to shout the name, reigning herself in or Cathal, and the bartender, would think she's a right lightweight.

"That's the one. My mate Billy knew him from school. He used to get us tins from the offie. Nothing serious, like. Just a few Kopparbergs or something. Of course, we were so young we thought we were steaming."

The two share a laugh again.

"That's why I feel like I've seen your face before. Brooke Park?"

"Aye, I used to hang around there all the time. Me and my mates. I remember your crowd. You were a few years older, but I used to fancy the fuck out of your friend."

Ava is taken aback for a split second. Cursing always shows how comfortable you're getting with someone.

"Blonde hair... Glasses..."

"Dearbhaile?"

"That's her. She was so hot."

"Aye, all the boys fancied her."

Their chuckles slowly disperse, but they continue to stare at each other, although both eyes are filled with projected memories from simpler times.

"So, a journalist?"

Cathal shrugs.

"It was free to do in the Tech, and I thought, you know what? I could do this. Always been a bit of a nosy bastard. Why not do it for a job? I'm still studying, like. Don't start lectures for another two weeks. Three days a week. In The Letter twice a week for work experience, Mondays and Wednesdays. Only been in about a month."

"Good for you," Ava smiles and nods her head. "Good for you."

So that means, both yesterday and today, he hadn't been coming from just down the street, Ava realises. No wonder he's been late both times. Cathal drops his eyes to his phone resting on the table between them as it lights up with another message. He'd been getting a few over the past hour.

"Do you want to take some of those?"

"No, honestly. It's fine. I get regular updates from all the other rags," he laughs, "as well as Sky News and the likes."

"Busy man," Ava eyes him. "Look... Let me buy you dinner... As a thanks."

She hears the grunt of the chair legs as they scrape across the wooden floor, and before she blinks, he's risen and has his bag swung around his arm.

"No, I'm sorry. I can't. I have to get home. I've to make dinner for my little sister. She'll be starving. But thanks for this," he indicates the glass as he finishes the last few mouthfuls.

"Well... Thanks again," she stands gauchely.

"Of course," he extends his hand again. "And, if there's anything else. Don't be afraid to contact me. You've got my personal Twitter now. But... Er... You know what? Here's my number."

He scrambles around his jacket for a pen, before extracting it and writing clumsily on a napkin, having to redo certain numbers as the material tears. After several attempts, he hands it over to her. She gratefully accepts, blinking through the smile, ignoring the dampness. Though sweat or drink, she isn't sure.

"Anything at all, I'd love to be first contact," he nods at her and skirts out of the room after a hurried goodbye.

Finishing her glass, Ava decides she's too far gone to drive. Thinking against contacting Mark in case he asks stupid questions, gets unnecessarily suspicious or makes obscene accusations. She's already treading on thin ice. She rings a taxi from the office around the corner, who irritably informs her that it's still early.

*'There's plenty of cars waiting outside, love.'*

Toppling over to the bar, she asks to pay the balance of her tab. The bartender leans lazily against the sink, cleaning an extra deep wine glass.

"No need. Your boyfriend already took care of it," he nods towards the door.

A sudden sense of guilt floods over Ava, as she thanks him and hobbles out onto the street and down the incline towards the taxi office. Why would he do that? Did he think it was some sort of date? Did she make it out that way? Did she give off wrong signals? Or was he repaying her for the solid story he told her his editor had congratulated him on? Either way, Ava decides she's definitely not going to tell Mark anything about tonight, and thanks the heavens that he's tied up with this new building that he probably won't even bother to ask.

*In Too Deep*

Bradd Chambers

\* \* \* \*

We stayed outside for the whole night. Just talking. Every now and then, Phil or one of the girls would come out to check on me, before raising their eyebrows and rushing back inside. Maybe it was the liquid confidence, but I just opened up to him in a way I'd never done before. Not even with Robyn or Phil. We talked about everything. My recently deceased parents. How one died of a heart attack and the other followed months later of a broken heart. My career and aspirations. My future. He was a Protestant and he didn't care that I was Catholic.

  "This whole religion thing is just stupid," he'd said, lighting a fag. "There's enough hate in the world without something as stupid as this. Who cares if you go to Mass and I go to Church? I don't, by the way. Our real hatred should be going towards people that deserve it. Murderers. Paedophiles. All sorts of criminals. I hope I'm alive to see the day when saying your religion gets the same reaction as *'I'm hungry.'* In Northern Ireland especially. If someone asks you where you're from, you're afraid to say in case you find yourself on the receiving end of a lashing."

I listened to every word he said. Watched his lips as they formed the words. He was so smart. So articulated. So intuitive.

Towards the end of the night, he walked me to a taxi and asked if he could see me again just as I was stepping into one. I panicked. He wouldn't like me. The real me. The uptight bitch with the hair in a bun without a litre of vodka down my gullet. He never waited for an answer anyway. He kissed me until the taxi driver blared his horn, asking if I was getting in or not. Leaving him, I asked to go straight to Robyn's. I didn't care that it was nearly one o'clock in the morning, I had to tell her.

"Fiona, what the hell are you playing at you eejit?" Robyn answered the door all bleary eyed and bed-headed.

"Rob," I grabbed her hand wiping the sleep from her eyes and squeezed it tightly. "I've met the man of my dreams."

Her eyes expanded. I never had time for boys. I stayed well clear of them, if anything. So this was a shock for her. And I never turned up to her house pissed. I barely drank.

We sat up all night laughing and talking, she even cracked open a bottle of wine. She said she was happy for me. She wished me well. But shortly after, it happened. The inevitable. What always happened the very few times when Robyn and I got drunk together. We cried and clung to each other. Reminiscing about our parents and the year we've had since their passing. We raised our glasses to them and talked about what we would do to honour them. That is, until Damien shooed us to bed, calling us a pair of clampetts for waking him up.

Bradd Chambers

# Chapter Sixteen:

Surprisingly, Mark rings halfway through the taxi journey home, just when they're pulling left at the Culmore Roundabout.

"Hi, babe."

"How've you been?"

"Aye, grand."

"No more worrying about those bloody shoes?"

Ava gives a fake laugh.

"No, no. Put it behind me," she lies.

To be honest, with the recent excitement of today, it had been in the back of her mind, but this gentle reminder has shoved it right back to the forefront.

"So, it wasn't Michael who bought you them?"

"Apparently not..."

Is this some sort of sick joke? Will he finally admit to it?

"Well... Must have a secret admirer then," he chortles. "Or it was the wrong address?"

"It wasn't the wrong address. Unless someone else in Woodbrook is called Ava."

"And is there?"

Ava lowers her voice as she sees the taxi man leer in through his rear-view mirror, no doubt fishing for gossip.

"I'm sure there probably is, aye."

"Then just be thankful ASOS or whoever delivered it to the wrong Ava," he laughs.

"But it-"

She bites her tongue. She doesn't want to tell him that it was hand delivered. She doesn't even know why she's opened the flood gates again, never mind giving another reason to make her seem crazy.

"Anyway, babe. Have you had a drink?"

Her heart feels like it's stopped beating.

"Er... Yeah. Why?"

"Can tell by your voice, just."

She relaxes.

"Yeah, went out for drinks after work. Why not, right? It's the weekend after all. And after the success of the story..."

She had briefed Mark fleetingly by text about the article.

"Oh, Ave. I knew there was something I was supposed to do. Look, the corner shop's still open. I'll run down and gra-"

"No, Mark. Honestly, it's fine. I have a copy here and there's a few more in the office. Going to get one framed and stuck on the wall. You'll have an opportunity. Don't get out of bed."

She listens as attentively as her tipsy brain can handle about his day as the taxi indicates right into Woodbrook, off the Lower Galliagh Road. She remembers getting lost the first time she came in here. Her friend, Molly, used to live just down the street from where she lives now. Before she pissed off to England for uni and never looked back. Met some rich Cockney and lives with him now outside Luton. She met up with her a few Christmases ago, more out of politeness than actual willingness. Their lives had gone two different ways, but that's what happens when you grow up. She had used to be in complete awe of the houses here.

Not that she could claim poverty. Her and her mother lived in quite a nice house just off the Springtown Road. She wasn't spoilt, but her mum wouldn't see her stuck. New uniforms every August, and nice treats from the town every payday weekend to keep her happy. What she wouldn't give to go back to those days.

"Ave?"

She snaps out of her daydream.

"Yeah, that sounds great, babe. Sorry, I'm just pulling up to the house now, give me two seconds."

She fishes a few fiver notes from her purse, paying and thanking the driver, before stepping out and clopping up her drive.

"Sorry, what were you saying?"

"I was saying the guy, Paul, from work invited us to a function tomorrow night at the City Hotel. Some charity fundraiser for kids with cancer. He knew you'd be up for it, and it'd be good to invite some big shots to your event on Wednesday. What do you think?"

As she clicks off her shoes at the door, she finds it hard to stifle a groan. People with loads of money barely give to charity. They'd rather invite a lot of people and pay as little as possible, so they can just stand with fancy clothes on and talk about their latest holiday to Bermuda or the new car they've bought.

But it was nice of Mark to think of her and her charity in that way. He's always been much smarter than her. She instantly feels guilty for feeling that way about Mark's friends. They'd been charitable towards her in the past, and so had Mark and his family. Just because they like the finer things in life doesn't make them bad people.

"That sounds great. Thanks, hon."

"You're welcome. You home now?"

"Yeah, just going to throw on some chicken and head to bed with a film," she holds the phone against her ear with her shoulder as she clatters into the kitchen, turning the big light on.

"Sounds like fun... Or... I could come over? I'm not meeting Dave until lunch time tomorrow. I could make you breakfast in bed, or we could go out..."

Ava doesn't hear the rest of his invitation.

"Aye. Babe... Please, get here as soon as you can."

"Great, just gonna get a shower and th-"

"No, shower here. Just... Please. Get here soon."

"Ave... What's wrong? Are you-"

Ava hangs up the phone and places it on the counter, her hand shaking vigorously. Moving over to the double French doors leading out into her elegant back garden, she violently shakes the key until it clicks, bursting onto the patio. Dropping to her knees, tears in her eyes. There, just outside the door, lies the Londonderry Letter, folded open at page 6. And sitting on top of the picture of her mother is a single lily. Her mother's favourite flower.

# Chapter Seventeen:

"What does this mean? Is it a threat? Someone trying to get me to shut up? I'm so confused, Mark... Mark? I'm scared. What am I going to do?"

Ava laps her kitchen table, occasionally pulling her chair out and back in again, deciding against sitting down. The hangover prematurely setting in. Mark's still on his haunches at the open doors, gazing down at the surprise.

"Ave... I don't think it means anything? Maybe one of your neighbours? Or friends? Or Robyn? Maybe they seen it and didn't want you to miss it?"

"But how would they know my mum's favourite flower, Mark? And around the back? Why around the back? Perfectly good step out the front. And they'd have to have came in through the back gate. Oh... They were in my garden. What the fuck, Mark. They were in my garden!"

Fresh tears spring to her eyes as she clutches the wooden chair, biting her lip to stop her sobs overcoming her. Mark groans lightly as he stands, a few bones cracking, before crossing the room and pulling her in for a hug.

"There, now. Babe, it's okay, it's okay."

"It's a threat, Mark."

"Who would want to do that?"

"I don't know. Boyle? Or members of his party, or supporters?"

"I very much doubt they'd leave a flower, Ave-"

"But they would. That's their intention. To shut me up!"

"... With a flower?"

She pulls away from him and gazes out of the window. She sounds insane. She knows she does, but she can't fight the feel of unease that's battering at her chest.

"I want to call the police."

She turns to see the expected look of shock etched across Mark's face.

"Now, c'mon. Ave, don't be too hasty."

"I'm not. I should've done it days ago."

"Days ago? Why? What's wrong?"

"With the shoes, I didn't order them, Mark-"

Mark slacks his neck, desperately trying not to roll his eyes as he looks away, his jaw clenched.

"- And they weren't delivered. Do you know that? There's no postage anywhere on them. They were left outside my door, just like these were," she flails her arms towards the patio doors.

Mark observes her a moment as she calms down. Nodding, he slides over, taking her hands and lowering them both into chairs facing each other.

"Look, Ave. I know you've been through a lot. You're going to be sensitive to these kinds of things. But, please, believe me when I tell you.

You're overreacting just a little. This is no big deal. You expect the worst in every situation, which isn't a bad thing 'cause you think of what could happen. But it can be hard to switch off sometimes. I understand that. But... Babe, anyone could have done this. It's not a threat from the politicians or anything like that, I promise you-"

"How could you possibly know that?" Ava almost chokes on her tears.

"I just do, Ave. You hear about stuff like that happening through the grapevine. People I work with get threats all the time. Nowhere near as nice as this. Threats are disgusting and vile. Like dog shit or fingers or something."

Ava fights the urge to tell him he's been watching far too many TV cop dramas.

"This was someone trying to help, I promise. So was the someone with the shoes. Hell, you know what states Robyn can be in sometimes, I can guarantee you that she's just forgotten to mention it to you."

Ava starts to take deep breaths, trying her best to snap out of the panic.

"Her car... It isn't in the drive."

"Was it here this morning?"

"Aye..."

"Well, there you are. She probably came over to get her car, and seeing that you were out, left the paper at the door with a lily. She knows they were her favourite flower."

Robyn had been incredible at the memorial service. Organising everything and knowing what she would've wanted in a way only a sister could have. Ava was useless.

"You're right, you're right," Ava smiles, wiping her eyes.

"And the shoes?" he continues, rubbing her leg reassuringly. "Sure, that's probably why she landed later that night. To ask you what you thought of them. And you saw the mess she was in. She probably didn't remember bringing them here herself."

Ava nods and beams at him, pulling him in for another hug. She doesn't dare mention the fact that the empty box lay in the living room for hours, a key to jog Robyn's memory. Or remind him that the note was signed *'M.'* He's trying his best to calm her down, and he probably believes all this himself. But she doesn't. She knows deep, deep down... Something's wrong.

# Chapter Eighteen:

Mark keeps his promise of breakfast in bed the next morning. Ava finally managed to dose off at around 6am, and just after 11 she's awoke with kisses on her forehead. Grumbling, she pulls herself up until her back is against the headboard, her eyes still struggling to cope with the light. Something heavy is placed on her lap. Yawning and wiping the sleep from her eyes, Ava looks down to see the feast on her mother's old dinner tray.

Her mum used to always watch TV in the living room. She was mad about all the quiz shows, making sure dinner was always ready before they started in fear of missing one. She said she dreamed of going on one one day. The board is stitched comfortably on top of a padded red checked cushion, with brown sauce stains still embedded into it no matter how many times they'd both washed it.

On top of the tray sits a wine glass of orange juice that she knows is about two weeks out of date, blackened toast with clumps of butter resting on top and a poor man's fry with two, still too pink, streaks of bacon and a solitary burnt sausage. Mark has his strengths, but culinary expertise is definitely not one of them. She smiles regardless and is about to thank him when she notices it. Propped inside a weathered measuring jug half filled with water is the lily from last night. It's lobbed slightly in her direction. Almost as if it's looking at her.

"Oh, hon. Thank you," she doesn't take her eyes off the lily. "It's lovely."

"I never thought you were going to waken," he smiles, plopping himself down on the bed beside her, a half-eaten slice of toast in his hand.

"I've barely slept the past few nights," she picks up her fork and wonders what looks the most edible.

"How are you feeling today?" his eyes transfixed on her.

"Aye... A little better," she lies.

"Good," he smiles, crunching the last of the toast with his teeth, crumbs falling unceremoniously onto her sheets. "Well, sleepyhead. I've to start getting ready for this lunch soon, so eat up."

He jumps up and heads for the shower. Picking up the sausage as the lesser of three evils, she bites into it and suppresses a gag. It's raw on the inside. When she hears the shower and the radio turn on, she slides the tray off, hops out of bed and reaches for the wicker bin in the corner. Lifting out the Tesco bag from within it, glad that there's only a few lashes that were unsuccessful in sticking to her own in there, she dumps the lot into the bag, before tying it up and lobbing it in the back of her wardrobe. Picking up the wine glass, she frantically searches the room, deciding the window is the best option. Thankfully, grass is below her window, so he won't see any wet patches when he leaves, as she chucks the juice out.

That done, she decides now is as good a time as any. She couldn't do a lot last night as Mark was by her side for the majority of the evening, so now she has a tiny bit of freedom and a window of opportunity. Unlocking her phone, she searches for Dermott's name. She hasn't spoken to him since Christmas time, when he'd kindly texted her. She reads it now.

*'Ava. Wishing you and your family a v merry Xmas. I know it'll be hard around this time but you know we're all here for you. Let me know if you ever want to talk. D x.'*

She smiles at the memory. Mark and her were lying in her living room after finally getting around to buying a TV. He bought it for her but wouldn't even think of asking for the money. They were watching *Home Alone* and had mugs of hot chocolate. It had finally started to feel like home for her. Much more than at Robyn's house, as awful as it felt to think at the time. It was her own space. Somewhere new. A blank canvas. Memories to be made. Sending him a quick text, she tells him that she really needs to speak to him and sends her address just as she hears the shower turn off.

# Chapter Nineteen:

Cleaning the surfaces of the counters for the fifth time, Ava busies herself with making every watermark invisible. The house is spotless, but she can't do anything but clean. It stops her worrying.

Dermott tried to ring twice once Mark came back into the bedroom from the shower. She hung up the first time right away, passing it off as a text. The second time she smothered it in her duvet. Luckily, Mark was too busy getting changed and talking about his meeting to notice. When he was leaving, he asked her again if she was alright.

"Just coming to terms with things," she smiled at him, knowing he wouldn't pry at the front door or he would be late.

He gave her a kiss on the cheek and squeezed her hands.

"Remember, be ready for half six tonight. Not a minute later, okay?"

She nodded.

"It'll give you a chance to wear that sexy red number you've been saving up," he raised his eyebrows and clicked his tongue.

She strained a smile and waved him off. When he was out of sight of the living room window, she checked her phone to see a text from Dermott confirming he'd be there soon. He just lives in Culmore, so it wouldn't take him long.

Now, she sits on the sofa in clear view of the window and her drive, perched on the end so she can jump up straight away once she sees his car. He arrives moments later, her frantically fixing her hair in the mirror above her fireplace. Like that would really make much of a difference. But if she opens the front door all wide eyes, tasselled hair and manic looking, it won't help her case.

She counts to three after he presses the door bell, before prepping herself and crossing the hall to the door. She smiles sweetly at him as he towers over her. At six foot three she's sure he towers over most people. His hair has more grey inching its way up from his ears than the last time she saw him. Although his eyes have more lines around them, they're still smiling down at her.

"Ava," he reaches for her hand and squeezes it instead of shaking it.

She steps back to let him through the threshold and he gazes around at the tiny hallway.

"This looks lovely. When did you move in?"

"The start of December."

"I like what you've done with the place," his voice booms as he saunters into the kitchen.

Typical policeman, can encapsulate a whole room and doesn't feel at all awkward in a new space. She follows, pouring water from the pre-boiled kettle into giant mugs.

"Oh, none for me, thanks," he holds up his hand as she reaches for the sugar jar. "Trying to cut down," he taps his belly as it sinks over his belt.

She smiles back. He had always been a bit on the heavy side, what with the number of takeaways and ready meals with the stressful and time-consuming job he had faced for the better part of forty years. But now, it seems retirement has taken its toll on him.

"It's the lack of exercise," he sighs as he dips into a chair at the table. "It drives me mad. I tried to join the gym down at Strand Road. But all those Adonis wannabees taking videos and pictures of themselves made me sick. Can't you go and better your health without telling the whole bloomin' country?" he shakes his head.

Ava nods along. Her social media is packed with those kind of lads, and ladies too. He thanks her as she hands over his mug and winces as he raises it to his lips.

"Too hot? Do you need more milk?"

"No, love. It's not that. It's just without sugar it seems pointless," he smiles across at her as she takes the seat facing him, her back to the patio doors.

At the head of the table sit the delivered box with shoes and note inside, right next to yesterday's Letter with the lily. He doesn't seem to notice the objects, and if he does, he ignores them.

"So, what made you want to move out of your Aunt Robyn's?"

Ava shrugs.

"I wanted a fresh start. Somewhere without any memories. I know I had the house in Springtown... But I could barely step foot back there to collect my things, never mind live there on my own. It was too hard. And with Robyn and Damien fighting all the time..."

She trails off, unsure how much she should say. It's okay talking to Robyn about it. She's family. Dermott isn't, no matter how much he feels like it.

"Yeah, I was sorry to hear about their split."

Ava gives a look that he knows is some unspoken thanks.

"So, formalities out of the way, why did you text me? Not that you can't, of course. I'm always on the other line for a chitchat. But it seems more sinister than that..." He narrows his eyes at her.

The normality of the conversation. It threw Ava. She almost doesn't want to tell him. Make up some stupid excuse that it had been too long. Or that she was lonely. But she can't do it. She has to know if there is something that can be done. Or if he knows something. Has heard something.

"I've been getting rather... Strange things left at my door."

Dermott's eyes expand. He straightens his back, fully attentive, back in work mode.

"Strange things? What kind of strange things?"

She bites her lip and tilts her head slightly to her left. Dermott gazes at the collection, going to reach out before halting.

"May I?"

"Of course."

Sensing something is wrong, he leans back in his chair and fishes out a pair of sterile gloves.

"You still keep a pair on you?" she can't help but guffaw.

"Hi, you never know when you're gonna walk in on a crime scene. I'll tell you that for nothing. And if not, they're always handy if the dog drops one at the side of the road," he winks at her, snapping the gloves on right up to above his wrist.

He lifts the lily first, the item closest to him. He turns it around in his hands, his face a mixture of curiosity and confusion. The paper's next.

"I haven't seen this one," his double chin prominent as he looks down his glasses at the story, holding it at arm's length.

"It was only in yesterday's," Ava sips her tea, bile in her throat.

He nods several times as he skims the story. After he's finished reading, he places the article down beside the flower and pulls the shoebox over. Lifting the lid precariously, he glances at the contents, lifting both shoes up and inspecting them before getting to the note. When he's finished, he pushes his glasses to the top of his head and raises an eyebrow at Ava.

"What are these?"

"I think they're threats."

"Threats?" he sounds astonished.

"Aye, they've only begun to come in since I've started being a nuisance in Darrell Boyle's plot to higher the railings on the new bridge. First the shoes came in on Wednesday, whether before or during our meeting I don't know as I left the house very early. I didn't think it was a threat then. But, I have the flower resting on the picture of my Mum's face last night when I get in. At my back door too," she thrusts her thumb behind her. "And lilies were her favourite flower. It just seems fishy..." She trails off as he re-examines the note.

"'M?'"

"I have no idea. I've thought of everyone."

"But why would they tell you they love you... If it was a threat? And why such expensive looking shoes? Albeit, they look a bit worn in. Second hand perhaps?"

"I don't know. To try and mess with me?" Ava decides against informing Dermott about the two occasions she had already worn them, ultimately taking the brand-new look off them.

"And how would they know your mother's favourite flower?"

"Her memorial service? I mean the place was littered in them..."

She rests her thumping head on a hand. He's already beginning to poke holes in her theory, and she doesn't blame him.

"I must sound mad," she laughs.

"You don't," he rests everything back down on the table and struggles to slide his gloves off. "You sound like a girl who has been through an awful lot. It's normal to see evil lurking around every corner after what you've been through. Believe me," he attempts to soothe her, but she can't take her eyes off the table, constantly picking at a dent in the wood.

"I guess I just haven't been getting enough sleep lately. And I've just been jumping to conclusions. Having nightmares. That kind of stuff," she sniffs, begging the oncoming tears to stop.

"It's only natural, Ava. You've built this charity out of nothing, and now Boyle, who I've worked with in the past and can honestly say is an egotistical twat," he spits out of the corner of his mouth, a hand pressed against his cheek like he's whispering about him in a crowded room.

Ava smiles and wipes her eyes.

"Boyle's bringing up trauma. Giving you, and the rest of the city, false hope. You want people to see what you're doing, and he's quashing that. It's obviously stirred up your emotions, which will always be there. Some sort of reaction in you that you didn't know existed. Your head's a bit all over the show at the moment. I'd take today to catch up on sleep. Get back into your jammies and get something soppy on the Netflix. Or a comedy you can fall asleep to. Don't be watching some horror film. That'll just make everything worse, for Christ's sake."

They both laugh and talk a while longer about her situation, the past, Robyn, Mark, before conversation turns to his retirement and his family.

A little over an hour later, when Dermott is standing at the front door, his shadow hiding Ava from the big bad world outside, she feels a lot better. All cried out and a few laughs. Probably just what she needed after a long hard week.

"I've to head on here, I promised Grainne I'd take her to Foyleside for some new dress she's been crying after," he rolls his eyes. "But listen, don't give any more of this another thought, you hear me? And I won't ring the boyos in the office and charge you with petty theft of those shoes," he sniggers.

He's right. Mark's right. She's looked far too much into this. Saw dark figures when there weren't any. He gives her a bear hug, making promises of always being a phone call away, before he marches out of the door and waves from his car. A lot more cheerful, Ava takes his advice and digs out the tub of caramel ice cream from the freezer, grabs a blanket and throws on a mind-numbing chick flick. She's already lost the most important person in her life, she won't lose anymore.

*In Too Deep*

Bradd Chambers

✳ ✳ ✳ ✳

The next morning, I woke feeling like my head had got run over by a double decker bus. Damien made us a good Irish fry, like the ones Da would make, before offering to leave me into town. I completely forgot that I had to open the shop after lunch. I groaned, hoping the shower would do me some good.

After a not so tactical vomiting session, I'd scrubbed myself as well as I could've without bringing off skin. Damien still said he could smell drink off me anyway. As he pulled up on the pavement at the bottom of Shipquay Street, I thanked him before stepping out of his car. Trudging up to the shutters, I jumped when I heard a voice beside me.

"Alright, gorgeous?"

Visibly startled, I turned and was surprised to see Chris slouched against the wall beside my store. A single lily in his hand.

"How did you..."

"Phil told me. We had a nice chat in the chippie after you left last night," he winked at me as I took the flower. "Never told me he was gay, now, did you? Trying to make me jealous?"

I stared at him dumbfounded.

"No," I laughed quizzingly.

"Well, anyway," he narrowed his eyes at me, "Phil told me you'd be opening today. I *did* ask if I could see you again... Eh?"

That cheeky crooked smile. The one that helped me fall in love with him and the one I would grow to hate.

"And from what I can remember, I didn't answer," I coughed awkwardly, blushing at the memory. "And... The lily?"

He looked at me with his lip protruded.

"What about it? Do you not like it?"

"No, I love it," I'd said.

How did you know it's my favourite? I wanted to ask him.

"Well, don't let me stop you from the jobs that need doing," he raised his eyebrows as Rachel slouched out of a taxi. "But, why don't you give me a ring?"

And with that, he took my hand, discreetly dropping a slip of paper with his number written on it, before pecking me on the cheek, turning away and sauntering up the street.

"Well... Looks like someone got lucky last night," Rachel nudged me.

I scowled at her.

"I did not. He just... Met me here this morning," I blushed again.

It sounded ridiculous.

"Aye, okay. I believe you. Now can you hurry up and open the shutter? I'm in dire need of a headache tablet."

Bradd Chambers

# Chapter Twenty:

Smiling at the door staff, Ava and Mark head through the open doors into the reception of the City Hotel. Immediately greeted with the wine-red theme of the upholstery of the hotel in the heart of the city, they trod through and up the stairs to the private function room.

After paying for their two tickets, they bypass the bar on their left to travel further into the room to be greeted by Paul, the guy from Mark's work. As the men speculate about business, Ava gazes around at the white washed table cloths fitted to the two dozen tables dispersed throughout the giant room, filled with fairy lights and the sound of the jazz band in the corner. She's bound to find someone she knows, but with everyone standing and moving about, she finds it hard to judge how many people are actually here.

"Awk, sorry," Mark turns and places a hand reassuringly on Ava's lower back, edging her into the conversation both physically and theoretically. "This is Ava."

Paul shakes her hand and gleams down at her cleavage a little too long, making her instantly uncomfortable and not a fan of his. Excusing herself politely, she marches straight over to the bar, ordering a gin and tonic and a small bottle of wine for Mark. Once ordered, she turns and inspects the people in the room again, her eyes finally settling on a purple dress with a sparkly brooch. But it isn't what she's wearing, it's who's wearing it.

"Kat," she exclaims.

Turning sideways with a smile, Kat's face instantly falls when she sees Ava. Chuckling nervously as she hobbles over, her clutch pressed against her stomach, no doubt to make her look a little thinner.

"Ava, hi. What are you doing here?"

"Mark's a friend of the organiser," she smiles at her. "You?"

"I'm actually dating his brother," she grimaces, pointing over at the man she was standing beside mere moments earlier. Ava can see a striking resemblance, hopefully he's not a perv too.

"I had no idea you were dating," she mocks punching her on the arm. "Good for you."

"Yeah, yeah. The boys are with their da this weekend, so I thought why not?"

"How long have you been seeing him?"

"Two weeks," she nods along, eyes expanded.

"That's a bit quick to invite you to something like this..." Ava bites her tongue.

It's none of her business.

"Sorry-"

"No, no. You're right. I agree," she sighs. "But after the stress with the kids, it's nice to let your hair down every once in a while."

They both smile and nod whilst Ava pays the barman. When she lifts the drink to her mouth and takes the first sip, she knows she'll have a glass in her hand all night.

"Well, nice to see-" she begins to pick up the glasses and bottle, before she's interrupted.

"Ava, I have a confession to make," Kat exhales dramatically. "I wasn't sick yesterday. Garrett-" she nods in the direction of Paul's brother, "- got me an appointment with a beautician. I got everything, and I mean *everything* done," she raises an eyebrow at Ava.

Ava smiles through her disgust. Is she imagining it or is Kat swaying her dress a little too awkwardly? She doesn't need to know about her bikini wax.

"Your eyebrows look lovely," she nods.

"That's not all. He got my hair done, it was a bastard to sleep in last night, and took me shopping in Debenhams. Debenhams, Ava. I only walk through there to get to Foyleside. No Primark for me tonight."

She definitely is swaying her dress now intentionally, forcing Ava to admire it.

"And today, he took me to get my makeup and tan done. He pulled out all the stops... And all I can think about is how I lied to you... Well, lied to Michael. When I should've been helping... I was off beautifying myself. I'm sorry."

Ava waves away her apology.

"There's no need to apologise. I would've understood. Just tell me the truth next time," she points her finger at her sternly before laughing.

It's a forced laugh, but not as forced as Kat's is. Through the gaggle of people, Mark finally rests his eyes on Ava and skirts over.

"There you are, thought you'd got lost with my drink," he smirks at her, reaching for his wine bottle.

After making introductions between Kat and Mark, Ava finally gets a respite to take another sip of her drink. The three discuss a bit about charities before the awkwardness becomes unbearable and Ava almost yelps with delight when Kat states she's going back to her date. But, of course, that means she has to socialise with more people.

# Chapter Twenty-One:

"Imagine the cheek of her," Paul shakes his head as everyone laughs along to his story, Ava managing a little chuckle to keep the peace. "And the worst thing about it? She's married to a politician over all people."

"Darrell Boyle?" the bald guy with the glasses far too big for him screeches hysterically.

"The very one," Paul flicks his drink towards him, spilling a little down his wrist. "It seems he doesn't give her a penny."

"She should have her own job and not rely on his wealth," a lady whose name escapes Ava says, scrunching her shoulders up and pouting in distain.

"I agree with you 100%," Paul nods, his blinking elongated, the whiskey definitely taking more of an effect. "What does that slabber do anyway? I saw him in the paper this week for something... What was it? Something to do with lifeboats or..."

"Increasing the height of the new bridge, or putting nets down," the first boy speaks again.

Ava fidgets uncomfortably, Mark moving slightly into her in his own way of protecting her, as if she couldn't hear them if he did so.

"That was it, that was it," Paul hiccups. "I mean, preposterous that there's anyone out there that has a problem with that, for Christ's sake. All those druggies that end up falling into the Foyle, or topping off it. Do the community a favour anyway."

A few people nod as he takes another sip of his drink.

"All a waste of energy, if you ask me. And the dole's money. And the emergency services. How can your life be that bad that you would rather swim with God only knows what at the bottom of that Foyle. The smell of it too," he titters, a few joining him.

"There was someone trying to openly stop him," another lady in a suede suit interjects. "Says that it isn't the right solution."

"And so they're right," Paul lags his head in her direction, although Ava believes he's that far gone he's not quite sure which woman said it. "Leave the beautiful picturesque view of our city alone. Instead, put a bullet in the stupid narrowminded heads of those who want to be in the front of the newspapers and trending on Twitter and Facebook so badly that they throw themselves off it."

At that, Ava shoves Mark's arm off her, not caring that she accidently knocks him into Paul, and hurries to the toilets, angry tears stinging at her eyes.

# Chapter Twenty-Two:

Bursting into the bathroom and slamming the cubicle door shut, she sits and lets the silent tears fall. Bastards like that are the narrowminded ones, she thinks. Just because he grew up with wealth and status, he thinks anyone dealing with mental health issues are instantly drug users.

She can't believe what she's just heard. She can't believe she let him away with it. She has half a mind to march back out there and make a scene. Throw a drink in his face. Scream all the accusations running through her head right now... But that would ruin Mark's night. Potentially taint his career. She isn't going to be *that* girlfriend, especially after the past few days.

She gets to work on her makeup, drying her eyes and adding a little more to conceal the fact that she had been crying. Just as she's about to stand up, she hears the door to the bathroom opening and two women walk in. She immediately recognises the voice of the woman she was standing with. The woman whose name she couldn't recollect.

"Aye, she's Fiona McFeely's daughter. Remember? Your woman who topped herself three years ago?"

"The name rings a bell..."

It's the second woman who had been joining in on the conversation with the suede suit.

"Oh, come on, Rochelle. There aren't many women who take their own lives, now are there? Especially at her age."

"Well, regardless, what about her?"

"That's why she stormed out. He was saying those things and she couldn't deal with it, obviously."

"But they were the truth?"

"I know that, darling. Everyone knows that. But you can't throw it in her face like that."

"And it was her who was petitioning to stop the expansion?"

"Yeah, she had a meeting with him and her gob was flashed across the Letter yesterday. Honestly, how do you not keep up with local news?"

"It doesn't interest me, Grace. It's no *Downton Abbey,* now is it?" Rochelle giggles.

The two ladies continue their laughter and mutter torts like *'selfish girl,'* just as Ava flushes the toilet and clicks open the door. They're stood at the mirror reapplying their lipstick, and when they both see her they halt, eyes widening, mouths open. Coughing politely, making sure they see her staring at their reflections, Ava marches straight past them and out the door.

# Chapter Twenty-Three:

Hammering back down the stairs, she sends Mark a quick text to let him know that she is getting a taxi home and to not bother coming after her.

*'Enjoy your night xx'* she adds to ensure he knows she isn't angry at him. Just as she's about to put her phone back in her bag, she looks up to come face to back with someone waiting by the doors. However, she's moving too fast and isn't able to stop on time.

"I'm sorry. I'm so, so, so sorry," she holds both hands to her head as he turns around. "Cathal?"

"We have to stop... Running into each other like this," he winks.

She manages to snigger lightly, despite her mood.

"What are you doing here?"

"Eoin, the photographer, had other plans. So muggins here has the job of coming and taking photos of the event upstairs. But I don't have my press pass, and the bouncer won't let me in without it."

"Dick!"

"No, no. It's not his fault. It's my own. My subconscious probably tried to forget it on purpose so I wouldn't have to do it. I'm a journalist, not a photographer. They're just getting me to do it as a scapegoat. Passing it off as improving my experience, when really they all have something better to do on a Saturday night. And to be honest with you, I don't have the money to spend on the taxi home, never mind getting in to take photographs. I'm sure they'll be on Facebook in the morning."

He wolf-whistles as he looks Ava up and down.

"Are you a member of the party?"

"I was, yeah."

Taken aback a little by Ava's bluntness, she apologises to him immediately.

"Sorry... It's just... Can I buy you a drink?"

# Chapter Twenty-Four:

A little over an hour later, they're already several drinks in. The commotion upstairs at the back of Ava's mind. Cathal managed to calm her down and they had a good rant about Paul and all his minions. Talking about different tragic or unfortunate circumstances they would love to see them in.

Ava has just stopped telling him about her mother, what a great woman she was. He smiles and fiddles with his glass. She clicks her head to the side to examine him, the drink forcing her to close one eye to see him better.

"Tell me about your ma, Cathal."

He shrugs.

"Not a lot to talk about."

"No, that's not true. Now my ma? That's not a lot to talk about. Not anymore, anyway," she smiles.

"I never met her," he begins to pick at the damp coaster. "She left shortly after I was born."

Ava's heart sinks.

"Oh... Cathal. I... I'm sorry."

"Never worry. You didn't know."

"What happened?"

123

"My da says it's 'cause she wasn't right. Always wanted something she couldn't have or be somewhere she couldn't get to. In the end, we weren't enough for her."

The familiarity of his confession hurts Ava's chest.

"We?"

"Me and my da."

"You mentioned a little sister last night?"

"Aye, Orla. She's only 14."

Ava nods, feeling like there's more to the story that he wants to tell. Reading his body language like she was taught in the counselling courses she took at the Tech before opening the charity.

"Yep... It's just me and her," he blows out, lifting his drink and draining it.

"Oh... Your da... Is he?"

He looks back up at her.

"As good as."

"Meaning?"

"Fucked off one day. Left me with her. I was only 15 myself."

Ava shakes her head, revulsion collecting in her stomach.

"I take it you went into care?"

"Nope," he shakes his head. "I couldn't do it to her. Or myself. I just pretended like nothing happened. Forged his signature on school documents. Said he was sick for parent's evenings. Luckily, he never showed his face around school much anyway, and his mate Jimmy works in the dole office, so he knew me well. I used to go in and collect it for him and take it to the bar or wherever he was that day. So, after he left... I just continued doing it. Nothing really changed that. Jimmy would just say *'tell him I was asking about him.'*

"Used the money on food and that before I got a part time job when I turned 16. Worked in the shop down the road from me. Then, when I turned 18, I started telling people he'd gone missing. Not for years, like. But acting like he hasn't come back from a mad weekend. Luckily, people around my parts don't ring the cops or ask a lot of questions, so it's grand. They still think he'll come back soon. Either way, I don't care. Now I'm the guardian of Orla... Not officially, anyway."

"And Orla's mum?"

"She left too. She was from Dublin. She went with my da for a while, but in the end... She just wanted to go home."

"That's sad. Did Orla know her?"

"Not really, she must've only been about three when she left."

"Were they together long? Your da and Orla's ma?"

"She never even lived with us. They just kind of saw each other when it suited them. She was an alcoholic. Used to hang around John Street, from what my da told me. I saw her there once. It was weird. She didn't even recognise me. That's how Orla came to live with us."

"And she doesn't try to make contact? With you or Orla?"

"Nope, just left one day and haven't heard anything from her since."

Ava shakes her head as he finishes his story. Seemingly everyone pivotal in Cathal's life has disappeared. How did he manage to cope? And with Orla under his wing?

"I can't believe you had the nerve to call me brave last night after everything you've been through. You should be so proud of yourself, Cathal. I'm serious," her tone turns dead as he snorts and looks away, making him glance back at her.

Their eyes meet for a few seconds and Ava questions whether this is a good idea. Especially after last night. Fresh guilt rising after him telling her about his money problems, then paying her drinks tab.

"Thanks," he coughs, standing.

Did he read her mind? Or was it something in her eyes?

"Just gonna nip to the bog here, be two ticks."

As she watches him leave, she pulls out her phone to see no new messages from Mark. Slightly pissed that he'd read the last one from herself, she forces down her annoyance. He needs to show his face, make more clients, do business. She wouldn't understand the politics of it all.

Tucking her phone away, she looks around at the downstairs bar area, smiling at people as she meets eyes with them. Turning almost 180 in her seat, she sees the same doorman standing at the door, looking a little bored. He's arguing with a drunken teenager, not letting him in. Some people have some nerve.

Just as she's about to turn back around she sees him. Mark. Scurrying across to the front door. She turns back in her seat again and presses herself as much as she can against the wall beside her, wishing she could just melt into it.

When the coast is clear, she fires Cathal a quick excuse through text, after programming his number into her phone last night in the back of the taxi, before trotting up to the bar and throwing two dog-eared £20 notes at the barman.

Did he see her? Is that why he left? She thanks God that he doesn't smoke or he would've walked right past her towards the smoking area. Checking that he's definitely not still outside, she jogs across the street, taking solace in the dark secluded car park, before sliding down Queen's Quay and rounding the back of the Guildhall, thumbing a taxi down from the bottom of Shipquay Street.

As she finally exhales and gives the driver her address, she tries to calm her beating heart. She isn't doing anything wrong. What does she have to feel guilty about? Cathal is just a friend... A work colleague. A member of the media to help with her business. She doesn't find him attractive in anyway. So why does she feel like she's betraying Mark's trust?

Bradd Chambers

\* \* \* \*

Chris and I were inseparable from then on in. The first date was sloppy, awkward and clumsy. The bowling didn't help. But I started to open up again after a few of the cocktails. I relaxed. And I let him kiss me again before I went home. Actually before stepping into the taxi, this time.

He changed something in me. I found myself strangely bubblier. Not that I was miserable to start off with. He just made me happy. Happier. He made me laugh like no-one I'd ever met before. Proper belly laugh until my sides were sore and I had to run to the toilet in fear of peeing myself. He was just my favourite person. I wanted to be around him all the time.

Everyone noticed the difference in me. The girls slyly giggling that all I needed was '*a bit*,' but it took us weeks to sleep together. It would've been longer, but I ended up getting really drunk and he brought me home in the taxi. I wouldn't let him leave. He refused to do anything, but he slept beside me, pushing me to the side every time I rolled over in case I was sick.

We did it the next morning. I woke up and saw him beside me, the memories flooding back.

But instead of being embarrassed, I found a level of respect for him that no-one else ever reached. I told him I loved him as he snored on, planting a kiss on his lips.

Of course, after that it was like clockwork. Daily. Cheeky phone calls during work hours. Rushing home knowing one of us would be waiting beneath the sheets. I'm not afraid to say he was the best I ever had. Not that the list was overly long. But those other boys were only after somewhere to fill. Chris nurtured me. Satisfied me. Made my toes curl. I genuinely felt like we were set for life. That was, until...

*In Too Deep*

Bradd Chambers

# Chapter Twenty-Five:

Robyn's face is bright as she steps aside to let Ava through her front door.

"Ave, it's so good to see you. But, you know you're more than welcome in this house. Any time. No doorbells. Just waltz in."

"I know, Rob. I just don't want to take you by surprise is all," she smiles.

In Robyn's condition, she can't be too careful.

"The only surprise I get is wondering who's at my door. I don't get much visitors, love."

She shuffles through the living room into the conjoining kitchen, Ava following at a safe distance. She gazes out at the impressive view from Robyn's living room window. The beautiful twinkle of the River Foyle in the summer's sun in the distance. The Foyle Bridge scaling across the water like a serpent, except for the several cement piers impaling the water.

She watches as dozens of cars speed across it, looking as small as ants from here. Going about their lives. Blissfully unaware of the ominousness of the river they cross to get from A to B. She remembers staring from this exact spot and watching the Foyle Search and Rescue patrolling the fastest flowing river in Europe. Looking for her mother.

"Your tea," Robyn nods towards the rickety table that has been plucked from a nest of three that have been part of this sitting room for as long as Ava can remember.

That's the good thing about Robyn. She's plain. Predictable. Doesn't like change. Maybe that's why her sister's death struck her so hard. She hasn't been the same since. Ava could see it from behind her eyes even when she was acting tough for Ava's sake. She walked in on her a few times looking at pictures of Ava's mother on her phone with a tissue pressed against her face. But once she saw Ava watching, Robyn jostled herself with making dinner or a hot drink, the sniffle the only inclination that something was wrong.

"How've you been?" Ava smiles over at her.

"A bit better, aye," she stretches her feet over the gold pouffe. "My tablets knocked me out for a good nine hours last night."

Ava wishes she could have such a luxury. Sleeping tablets only make her groggy, she has yet to try some that knock her out completely.

"How was the fancy shindig last night?"

Ava busies herself with dunking her digestive into the drink, sucking at the dissolving biscuit as it crumbles in her mouth. Still Robyn stares over, relentlessly.

"Was grand, aye."

Robyn's eyebrows raise.

"What happened?"

Ava sighs. She didn't come over to talk about what happened last night.

"Just some posh twats not having a clue about what they're talking about."

Robyn shifts her head to the side, an indication to continue.

"They were talking about my battle with Boyle. Basically, saying that it's a waste of time because everyone and anyone who jumps the bridge are on drugs."

Robyn's eyes expand as she struggles out of her chair, hurrying to the kitchen. Moments later, she reappears with two thick slices of apple tart.

"Freshly made this morning. Not by myself, of course. Got it down the road at the Spar."

Ava thanks her aunt. She always remembers requesting pies when Robyn babysat her. The sickly feeling she got when she secretly bit into a rhubarb one before dinner once, mistakenly thinking it was apple. Her comeuppance, Uncle Damien had called it.

Robyn returns to her chair and busies herself with talking about the TV programme she has on mute. Asking Ava if she's seen it, not bothering to wait for an answer as she depicts what the character on screen is up to. Ava nods along politely, her eyes moving from the TV screen and settling on the cabinet it rests on. The ornaments and picture frames. The one resting on the VCR of particular interest.

"Have you heard anything from Damien?" she asks when there's a lull in the conversation while Robyn takes a sip of her tea.

Robyn follows her gaze to the wedding picture, smiling gently.

"No."

"Where did he go, Rob?"

Robyn shrugs.

"Last I heard he was up and about around Letterkenny direction doing a bit of work."

Damien is a self-proclaimed business man who mastered all skills. You could call him and ask him about anything from electrical to plumbing. When Ava moved into her house, Damien was the first over to inspect it with her. Whispering to himself more than to her about what *'just won't do'* and what he could *'get fixed in no time.'* It had been a long five months since she'd heard anything from him.

"Don't you miss him?"

Robyn pretends she didn't hear her.

"I do," Ava admits, staring at her aunt.

Robyn sighs, wiping her eyes.

"What happened that night, Rob?"

Robyn looks longingly at her. For a second, she thinks she actually will find comfort in her niece. She's never told anyone the facts about that night. But she decides against it.

"I told you. Nothing critical. We were just not happy for quite some time."

"Was it because of Mum?"

Robyn jumps like she heard a gunshot.

"Don't be ridiculous. Of course it wasn't. And it had nothing to do with you either, before you think such silly things."

"It's just... When I lived here... Sorry, Robyn, but I couldn't help but overhear your arguments. The walls *are* thin."

Ava remembers the nights she'd lie awake, insomnia brought on by grief. She'd hear the whispered but heated conversations from the other room. Damien would call Robyn looped, tell her she needed help. But the next day at breakfast he'd be all smiles.

"Why did he leave you?"

Robyn stares at the TV again, shaking her head.

"He just... Wasn't a very nice man, Ave."

"Did he hit you?"

"God no, pet. You need to stop overthinking things. Things weren't right with us for a while. But we just kept it behind closed doors. Put up a front. You lived here for a few years, you obviously saw the cracks in the relationship. But they were there a long, long time. They weren't fresh."

Ava nods, knowing her aunt well. Knowing she wants this conversation to draw to a close.

# Chapter Twenty-Six:

"Well, I better get off," she stands after the forced small talk runs dry, leaving the fork on the side plate with a light clatter. "Mark's bringing over a Chinese tonight. I'm a bit hungover, so hopefully the curry sauce can do its wonders."

Robyn beams up at her as she too rises to her feet.

"Right, love. Well, don't be a stranger. You know you're always more than welcome here. Oh, I almost forgot..."

And with that, she skirts around the corner and up the stairs. Ava listens to the creaks of the ceiling, following the noises with her eyes before they come to a stop. She waits for several more moments before joining her. As she turns right on the landing, she sees Robyn sitting in her old bedroom. Well... Not *her* old bedroom, but Robyn's spare room that housed her for several years after her mother's death.

She stands under the threshold, examining the room and comparing it to the one in her old home. The home she shared with her mum. Her old room's walls were plastered with pictures of her and her friends, mirrors and fairy lights, posters of

Kanye West. These things never made it back onto the walls of this room. The lick of cream paint left untainted. Her eyes rest on Robyn perched on the side of the bed. Her hands submerged in an old shoe box. The merlot red heels flashing back unwantedly in her mind, Ava struggling to push them back down.

"I found this when I was cleaning up the other week. I thought you might like it."

Robyn finds what she's looking for and wields it in front of her. Ava takes it gratefully. A photograph of a much younger looking Robyn and Ava on the Portrush Harbour. Ava mustn't be much older than three or four. Green mint ice cream stains the front of Ava's *Barbie* top. Still she giggles on, Robyn's arms wrapped around her. A huge grin on her face. Ava's eyes rest on the shadow on the bottom right side of the photo. Her mother, behind the camera.

"Thanks, Rob. This is so nice."

"I found it amongst old things, put it in here for safe keeping. Thought you might like it," she beams. "Memories."

"Thanks, I'll find a frame for it and put it up. We hardly have any pictures together."

Robyn waves away the statement. She's always hated having her photograph taken. She makes a move to go out of the door, but Ava's attention lands on what was resting just behind where she sat seconds before. Obstructed by her body. Mr Ted. The teddy her mum won for her on the claw machines in Barry's Amusements the same day this photograph was taken. His ear looks a bit frayed from when Ava used to drag him around by it. But otherwise he's still in relatively good condition. All his eyes, paws and the original stuffing.

"You loved Mr Ted," Robyn says from behind her. "Why don't you bring him too?"

Ava gives herself a shake. She's 20-years-old. She doesn't need a cuddly toy.

"I'm fine. I know he's safe here," she winks back at her.

As they descend the stairs, Ava finally decides to quash her fears.

"This might seem weird, Rob. But can I ask you something?"

She's decided she'll ask her now when she's in good form. If these mysterious items aren't her aunt's work, she won't panic. But she just needs to know whether all that worrying was for nothing.

"Of course, darling. Anything."

"A pair of shoes landed at my door the other day. Addressed to me. You wouldn't happen to know anything about them, would you?"

Robyn turns to look up at her as she reaches the bottom of the stairs. Her face gives Ava the answer before she vocalises it.

"No, love. Should I?"

"Just trying to figure out who left me them, that's all," she smiles. "And on Friday when you came around to collect your car, you didn't happen to leave a copy of the Letter at my back door? Open at my mum's picture?"

Robyn looks taken aback.

"Of course not, Ave. You know I don't read the papers."

Ava nods, making her way to the front door.

"Didn't they leave a note?"

"Sorry?"

"The person who left the shoes? Left the newspaper?"

"Just with the shoes. It didn't say much, only *'I love you'* and signed *'M.'*"

Robyn's mouth falls open. Several seconds pass before she starts laughing.

"You takin' the piss?" she stutters. "I'm guessing it was Mark?"

"No, no. Mark denied it."

"Mark... Mark... Mark... Who's Mark? I know that name?" she presses a finger to her lips and gazes out of the window

Ava stares at her blankly.

"Mark? My boyfriend?"

She looks back at her and smiles.

"Don't know when Damien's back, do you, love? That boiler's been on the brink again."

# Chapter Twenty-Seven:

The smell of takeaway fills the kitchen as Mark busies himself with getting plates, forks and glasses of milk. Ava opens the foil cartons, moaning slightly as she licks the side of her thumb from the leakage of sauce. Plopping the fried rice and chips onto a plate, she takes the small satisfaction of covering her entire dinner with curry, the odd bit of chicken or pea splattering onto the scene.

Her own complete, she turns to Mark's, only to find it missing. Looking back, she sees him already sitting at the table, digging into his salted chilli chicken. Shrugging her shoulders, she slips the plate into her hand, exhaling heavily in sharp bursts at the heat of it. She'd had the plates resting in the oven whilst she waited for Mark's arrival. An odd habit her mum had passed down to her. Dropping it onto the table beside Mark's, she joins him, placing a hand on his leg.

"Thanks, Mark. I needed this."

He nods, slurping up stray noodles that fell from his fork. Is she imagining it, or is there tension? An atmosphere? She turns to see her own glass empty, his filled to the brim with milk. The carton's lid clumsily left on.

"Erm... Is everything alright?"

Mark nods again, picking at a pepper stuck in his teeth. Raising an eyebrow, she makes a start on her meal, not able to deny her groaning stomach the pleasure any longer. Ava questions whether to tell him about visiting Robyn. More specifically, that she denies sending the shoes. But something about his demeanour tells her that it isn't the right time, so they eat in silence

# Chapter Twenty-Eight:

When dinner is over, he scrapes the leftovers into the takeaway bag, before tossing it into the open bin. He fights with the hot water, jiggling his leg impatiently, waiting for it to heat up. When he's done washing his own, he marches over and snatches Ava's plate from her hands.

"Babe... Honestly? What's wrong?"

Mark stares into the sink, aggressively rubbing her plate with the brush.

"Mark? Talk to me?"

He physically tenses, the glass in his hand clinking off the side of the sink. His jaw finally relaxes as he turns to face her.

"Who were you out with on Friday night?"

Ava blinks several times, panic rising within her. Then she stops herself. She's done nothing wrong.

"A mate."

"You said you were out with friends," he emphasises the *'s.'*

"No, I didn't."

"You did."

"No, I told you I went out for drinks. You never asked me who with. Why?"

"Tom saw you."

Her face remains defiant.

"In the Icon. With another man."

She nods.

"And?"

"You aren't even going to apologise?"

"Why should I apologise?"

"You've been caught out."

"No, I haven't-"

"Crying onto me about all these presents being left at your door. Hiding text messages and phone calls. Me acting like I don't see it, like a dick. Too scared to offend you. Well, I'm not taking it anymore, Ava. I'm not. I'm no longer walking on eggshells around you. You've been through a hard time, I get that. I sympathise with that. But it doesn't give you the right to treat me like shit. I know everything!

"Tom sent me a picture of you with him on Friday night. Then you have the audacity to sit downstairs in the hotel last night with him and drink away. After completely embarrassing me in front of my work ones, and potential clients. But no, you'd rather sit and have a drink and a laugh with your man. Literally right under my nose.

"Aidan saw you when he went out for a smoke. Came up and told me you hadn't left at all. After me making some bullshit excuse about you not feeling well and wanting to go home. As if I wasn't embarrassed enough. You could've at least gone to a different bar, for fuck sake. Do I look stupid to you, Ava? Who is he?"

Ava stares at him, mouth open. So much information in such a short outburst. Mark grimaces.

"I can't even look at you," he makes for the door.

"No, Mark. Stop, please!"

But it's too late, he's already out the front door and making for his car. She watches from the step, silently willing and begging him to come back. There are still a few of the neighbouring kids out in their gardens playing, and the family two doors down are standing at the barbeque. She won't embarrass herself. Her stomach churns, and not with the hangover, as she catches the glare of his stare as he reverses out of her drive and speeds off, leaving her with a hollow chest and wet eyes.

# Chapter Twenty-Nine:

The next few days go by in a blur of frenzy in work and lonely nights at home. Mark won't answer his phone anytime she tries to ring him and hasn't responded to any of her texts. She has half a mind to show up at the Carlisle Road space but can't face the humiliation of seeing any of his work friends, if they know. And if they don't, she doesn't want them to witness the cold blank stare he would give her before walking away. She tried his house a few times, but he's either not been home or intentionally hasn't come to the door.

She sits on her laptop in the spare bedroom. She calls it the spare bedroom, but it's merely a box room with a tidy rail filled with her over spilling clothes from her wardrobe and a single desk plucked from an eBay seller's house just outside Greencastle. She jumps between Facebook and Twitter, reading and liking the comments about the fundraiser tomorrow.

She'd found it so hard the past two days to paint a smile on her face. Acting like everything was fine and the fundraiser was the next best thing. If she's honest, she would rather lie in bed all day tomorrow and let the other four coax their way through it. But she can't do that. She has to show her face. It's her day. Her mother's name. Her charity.

She's just after retweeting the guy who came fifth on *The X Factor* seven years ago, who has voiced his excitement on his verified Twitter account. Although he's from Omagh, he's agreed to come up tomorrow and perform a few songs. Hopefully he sings covers, she thinks, as none of his originals even charted. Not even in Ireland. That's when she sees the *'1'* beside the envelope, indicating a new personal message. She hovers over the name.

*'@heathermoore71.'*

She doesn't know a Heather Moore. Clicking onto the profile, she sees she has no followers, no tweets and no pictures. Probably some hoax. Trying to get Ava to send her money. Clicking onto the message to get rid of the notification, she looks at the simple two letters.

*'Hi.'*

Shaking her head, she clicks out of the message and back onto her homepage. Liking and retweeting a few more people excited about the fundraiser, she checks the time. It's almost gone 11pm. She needs to be up early tomorrow to sort out the event, held in St Columb's Park off the Limavady Road. There's so much to do and so many people to meet. She needs to sleep. A bottle of wine helped her doze off the past few nights, but after waking today with a splitting headache and an icky tummy, she decided she'd try going au naturale tonight.

Clicking her laptop down, she picks up her bottle of water and crosses the landing into her own bedroom. She goes about her night time routine, applying lotions and potions her mum used to swear by. And why not? The woman was in her forties when she died and could have still passed for her late twenties. The hairs on the back of her neck stand up as she pulls off her top, beauty regime complete. She registers the fresh goose bumps on her arms. Something isn't right. She flicks her head to the side, towards the window. The blinds aren't closed, and sway in the August breeze.

That's when she gasps. Something just moved. Right there, beside the street light. In front of the bushes. Rushing over and yanking the plug of the lamp out of the wall, no time for trailing behind her bedside cabinet for the switch. Sliding over on her haunches towards the window, she peaks over her dressing table. Out into the darkness. The night is still. The only sign of life coming from Mrs McVeigh's TV in the living room. She could've sworn she saw a dark figure right there, beside her bushes. In *her* garden. She weighs her options. Call Mark? He won't answer. The police? Dermott? They'd think she's mad. She sits there a while longer, but nothing short of the small tree on her lawn moves with the wind.

Finally admitting defeat some moments later, she climbs into bed. Only when she's safely below the covers does she take off her jeans, slipping into the pyjamas stashed safely below her pillow. She gazes out of her window for several more minutes before, adrenaline extinguished, sleep overpowers her. She turns her back to it, letting herself drift off. A ping in the darkness makes her eyes shoot open. At the foot of her bed lies her discarded phone. Reaching for it, intent on putting it on silent, she can't help but steal a glance at the notification on her screen. From Twitter.

*'@heathermoore71: good luck tomorrow x.'*

*In Too Deep*

Bradd Chambers

✳✳✳✳

It came as quite a shock that I fell pregnant. We were always careful. I started taking pills when I knew we were getting serious and we never had sex without a condom.

"These things can happen," the doctor explained when I went for confirmation, even though I knew within myself that I was.

As if that was supposed to make it okay that the contraceptives hadn't done their job. I thought of how I would break the news to Chris. We were exclusive, but we were only together for three, nearing four, months. We'd had our first fight. And our second. To be honest, I lost track of how many we'd had. The honeymoon period was over as quickly as it had started. Everything about me seemed to irritate him. He'd tell me all the time.

How was I supposed to drop a bombshell like this on him? I decided a trip away would be the best thing. So, marching into the travel agents, I booked us a B&B in Dublin, the last of my parent's will money spent, and went to surprise him outside his work.

He worked in the council buildings at the time. I waited outside, knowing he was finished at six. Shortly after half, he marched out, his jacket swung over his shoulder, laughing along with a woman in a revolting tweed skirt. When he saw me, his smile dropped. Excusing himself, he took my arm and led me away.

"What're you doing here?" he said sharpish.

"Who's she?" I eyed her territorially.

"Lindsay, a girl I work with. Anyway, that doesn't matter. What's going on?" he registered the envelope in my hand.

I brandished it in front of me, trying to bring the conversation back to a light discussion. Like we were in love. After opening the envelope and examining the print out, he scratched his moustache thoughtfully.

"This weekend?"

"Aye, you asked if we could do something?"

"Aye, on the Saturday," he looked over his shoulder again towards Lindsay, who was still standing where he left her, kicking stones across the pavement and out onto the road.

"I'm sorry... Er... I wanted to surprise you?" I narrowed my eyes at him.

"And that's nice and all... But..." He seen my grudging stare. "What's this really about?"

Lindsay coughed dramatically, only stopping when we looked over and composing herself with a fake '*excuse me.*'

Chris expanded his eyes at her, before turning back to me. Grunting with disgust, I stormed off, ignoring his calls as I started to cry in the middle of the street.

*In Too Deep*

Bradd Chambers

# Chapter Thirty:

The screams and laughter of kids reverberate across the field, primarily used for football in the centre of the running tracks. Hundreds of people have turned out to enjoy the evening. The bouncy castle wobbles with the mass of children inside, the owner having to stand at the front and dictate a one-in, one-out system for health and safety reasons. The sides of the pitch clogged with vans selling chips, burgers, kebabs and other festival style foods. The small stage at the top gathers the performer's fans, singing along to the rendition of *'Wonderwall'* blasting through the speakers.

Ava stands and examines her creation. What a success. Dozens of newly retired men and women and homemakers with their kids going to school in September have approached her to say they want to volunteer when the new space opens. Whether with admin or a listening ear, it's all more than Ava expected. Much more.

Her eyes settle on Robyn, who staggers towards her and her heart drops. She did say she was going to call over, but Ava didn't expect her to be drunk. Hurrying over towards her aunt, she fakes a smile before linking arms with Robyn and twirling her around towards the steps and back up to where she came from, Browning Drive.

"Robyn, you're plastered!"

"Am I fuck," Robyn hiccups. "I just went for my lunch over the town and had a few glasses of red before tottering over to see you."

She attempts to pull away from Ava, turning her top half in the direction of the fundraiser. But Ava strives on, dragging Robyn's wonky, jelly-like body along with ease.

"Lunch? It's past seven o'clock, for Christ's sakes. You need to leave. Everything's going well. I can't have..."

Her voice falters as they reach the top of the incline, the carpark in sight.

"You can't have – me embarrassing you?" Robyn mutters.

Ava's heart sinks.

"Look, Rob... This is a big deal, okay? If you were sober, of course you'd have been welcome. But no... I can't have any drunk people at this. It's family friendly. I've already had a few side-eye complaints about there not being a bar here. Please, Robyn. I need you to leave. I'll come over and talk later. For Mum's sake?"

She knew she'd pressed the right button before she had even said it. But she can't feel guilty. Nothing can go wrong. Not tonight. Tears collect in the corner of Robyn's eyes.

"For your mum... I... I did have a contribution, but..."

Ava shakes her head, both with acceptance and annoyance, and goes to soothe Robyn before she stumbles forward. But instead of heading up the drive towards home, she crosses the road and heads for Ebrington Square, en route to the Peace Bridge which will allow her access over to the Derry side once more.

The Peace Bridge is a footbridge across the River Foyle that was opened in the summer of 2011 in a desperate attempt to bring unity between the predominantly Catholic Derry side and the primarily Protestant Waterside after a troubled past. Ironically, there have been spats of sectarian attacks on and around it to make the local community wonder whether the £14 million development was even worth it. Despite this, it attracts countless number of tourists and helps decrease parking in the city centre.

When Robyn finally reaches the corner and disappears from sight, Ava returns to her charity night. Stepping down the first few steps, she casts another nostalgic overview of the area, only to gasp when she sees who is lurking in the shadows of the hot dog van.

# Chapter Thirty-One:

Taking the steps two at a time and marching across the field, her scowl prominent despite the throng of people, she spits venomously when she reaches the hideaway.

"What the *hell* are you doing here?"

Darrell Boyle breathes in, bringing himself to his tallest, which isn't very effective at five foot nothing.

"Free country, isn't it, McFeely?"

Ava narrows her eyes at him, very aware of the people around her. No one has given them a second glance... Yet. She instantly turns to work mode.

"Of course it is, Boyle. But why would you come to such an event? I don't condone fox hunting, so I wouldn't go to a fundraiser to support keeping it lawful. I'm merely asking of your intentions here?"

Boyle smirks discreetly.

"Clever girl. I never thought that about you, you know that? You might be young and innocent looking... But the woes of the world have lit a fire in you. A fire I admire, if I'm honest."

His eyes sparkle as he talks to her, leaning forward ever so slightly until she can feel his breath in her face.

"There's no need to go through all this trouble, you know? Getting Z-listers and pizza vans infested with salmonella on your side. Just to make a bit of extra cash and to prove a point to me. We want the same thing, you and me."

Bile rises in Ava's throat.

"We definitely don't."

"No?" Boyle raises his eyebrows. "We want to stop people committing suicide. We should be on the same team here, shouldn't we? Could be..." He winks. "Partners."

Ava makes a guttural sound.

"I would never be partners with the likes of you."

Boyle's gaze travels down to her top, her breasts bulging out as she stands defiantly. She sheepishly wraps her jacket tighter around her. Boyle looks back into her eyes with an even bigger grin. Almost as if he won.

"You know... My wife's away this weekend. I'll have the house all to myself... If you wanted to-"

"Darrell Boyle, I didn't expect to see you here."

Darrell visibly retreats back a few inches and turns to the intruder. Ava has never been so happy to see Cathal.

"You know," Darrell clears his throat dramatically. "Just eyeing up the competition."

His eyelid closest to Ava flickers as he smiles professionally.

"Lovely to see you again, Ava. And good luck with all this," he wavers his hand towards the pitch as a whole before turning and sauntering further into the park, leaving Ava, Cathal and the rest of the fundraiser in his wake.

Ava and Cathal watch him go before finally resting their eyes on one another, each smiling slightly.

"You came?"

"Of course. Sorry I'm a bit late. I tried my hardest to persuade Orla to come, but she's getting big now. Doesn't want to be seen with her older brother. I thought a few friends from school would be here, but turns out they'd rather hang out outside the library on Foyle Street instead."

"No need to apologise, although it would be much better if your sister was hanging out inside the library rather than out."

The two share a laugh.

"I... I'm sorry about Saturday night, Cathal. Mark came down and saw me and asked if I wanted a lift home. He'd ordered the taxi already and it was sitting outside. I tried to wait for you, but the driver was an impatient ol' bastard."

Why is she lying? Cathal nods along regardless.

"Mark?"

"Aye, Mark..."

Oh, my God, Ava thinks. Has she really never mentioned Mark to Cathal? This makes her seem even more deceitful.

"My boyfriend."

The alarm in Cathal's face can't be subdued.

"Oh... Right. Well, that's no worries, Ava. I was there for work anyway. My editor wouldn't have been happy if he'd have known I was sitting having drinks with you instead," he chuckles.

It all sounds so innocent, but yet...

They gaze around them, taking in the scene, and shift uncomfortably. Their eyes occasionally meeting, an overly eager smile on both of their faces. Each one goes to say something and stops, before repeating the same transaction.

"You go," Ava points at him lazily.

"Speaking of work, I best be off. Taking pictures again today, but also doing a bit of a colour piece. Going to talk to a few people as well. Could I steal a quote from you later?"

"Of course you can," Ava nods at him as he shifts off into the crowd, taking in the sweat patches below his armpits and down his back that she didn't notice before.

# Chapter Thirty-Two:

Wandering aimlessly around the pitch, Ava smiles towards people she'd know to see, and exchanges pleasantries to strangers who know of her. Infamous in the city. No longer a face in the crowd. Her smile drops every time she thinks she isn't being examined, which isn't very often. She's the star of the show. Passing the arts and crafts tent, she's shocked to see her standing there.

"Ava!" Zoe pulls herself away from the table where she had just finished painting whiskers on a toddler's face.

"What are you doing here?" Ava welcomes the hug whole heartedly.

"Just volunteering, the usual," she winks at Ava. "This is incredible," she says, surveying the scene.

"Aye... Great turn out," Ava smiles, turning and looking at her masterpiece.

The silence grows awkward. Like it always does.

"How have you been?" Zoe says the inevitable.

"Grand... Grand. Just keeping busy with all this, you know? And you?"

164

"Aye, I'm okay..." Zoe bites her lip.

Ava's seen it before. They never want to say they're more than okay or bring forward good news involuntarily. It's like Ava's a wounded animal who will pass away at the prospect of someone else's life going better than her own.

"How's Ronan?"

"All good... In fact..."

She blushes as she pats her stomach, her teeth clenched in an awkward smile.

"You are not!"

"Aye... Four months."

They embrace once again.

"I'm so happy for you."

"I know. It's so weird. It wasn't even planned. I thought Ronan was going to leave me when he found out," she laughs, making Ava's eye twitch slightly in shock. "He always said he hated kids. Wanted nothing to do with them. But now... I don't know. He was over the moon. I always said to him it'll be different when it's his own. So, here's hoping," she crosses her fingers as she brings them up to her cheeks, happy tears in her eyes.

"I wish you all the luck in the world," Ava tries to bring the warmth of her smile to her eyes, but she's afraid she'll be given away. "I'll leave you to it," she directs her head towards the queue of kids waiting. "Thanks so much for coming and please, don't be a stranger."

The irony of the statement isn't lost on her as she trudges off, eager to escape, sure she'll be avoiding the crafts tent for the rest of the night.

Zoe is a volunteer with the Foyle Search and Rescue. Foyle Search and Rescue is a charity in the city set up over 20 years ago to target the increase of deaths by drowning and suicide in the River Foyle. Zoe was on call the night Ava's mother jumped. She was still very young, in her early twenties, at the time. She sympathised with Ava immediately as she'd lost her own mother to cancer at a similar age. Zoe was Ava's source within the group, and often after an unsuccessful search she would land to Robyn's house for a chat and a cup of tea. Reassuring Fiona's remaining family that they were doing everything they could to find her body. Unfortunately, with it being the middle of winter, and the water close to freezing, the chances of a body resurfacing anytime soon were slim.

Afterwards, when the search was finally called off, Zoe still visited Ava a couple of times a week. Sharing intimate memories of their mothers. But, as what happens many friendships, life intervened. There were times Zoe was contacted during her visits to say she was needed on the boat. The visits dwindled to a few times a month, to once every few months. Then, eventually, she stopped visiting altogether. Tonight was the first time Ava had saw her in close to a year, although there was the odd Facebook like and comment.

Ava doesn't hold Zoe responsible for being unable to find her mother's body. Nor for her not being a main priority in her life anymore. It would be terribly foolish of her, considering the number of people entering the river every year. But seeing her genuinely happy and beginning to start a family of her own, moving on with her life... It struck a cord in Ava. A selfishness that she couldn't hide, wishing she could do the same.

Zoe had her mourning. She had the weeks and months leading up to her mum's death to get herself in the mind frame that she was never going to be at her wedding. Or at her bedside when she was giving birth. Zoe had kissed her mother's cold face goodbye at the funeral. Of course, everyone told her that even if her mum's body was found, there would be no way Ava would ever be able to do such a thing. But it still stings. It's made her feel like she'd not moved forward in the past three years. Living life like a zombie whilst everyone moves on with theirs. Like she was stuck in slow motion. Now, with Mark not speaking to her, and the recent depression and paranoia kicking in, it feels like she's taken a step back, if anything.

Realising she's at the edge of the pitch, just beside the houses overlooking the night, she turns and stands by the stage, surveying everyone's cheery faces. Singing along. Laughing with friends. Exchanging gossip. All eyes bright with excitement. They've all come tonight for a good cause. She wouldn't be ungrateful and say they haven't. But how many of them have truly felt how she's felt? Lying awake at night wondering why she wasn't enough? Why her mother felt so awful that she would leave her only daughter alone and scared in the world at only 17-years-old? What she could've done to make her stay? To stop her?

Instead of having a stupid argument before slopping to bed. Throwing pillows and big heavy jumpers under the covers in the shape of a human. Climbing out of her window and perilously crossing the garden, her mother's back to her as she watched the TV. Ava's last ever image of her. Just the back of her head inching out from above the sofa. If she could only go back in time and leave meeting Mark in the car to another night. She'd rush back in through the front door and embrace her mother. Tell her she loved her. Force her to stay. Barricade the doors. Ring an ambulance. A doctor. Robyn. Anyone who could talk some sense into her. Make sure she didn't leave her.

All these unanswered questions that she'd had running around her head ever since that night. Questions that will never be answered. She wipes the tears collecting in her eyes as she forces a smile, making her way back into the crowd. Determined to make her proud.

# Chapter Thirty-Three:

Smiling towards the phone in *The X Factor* alumni's manager's hand, Ava had been oddly confused when he had asked her for a *'selfie.'* But now as she stands with his arm draped around her shoulder, she realises the true intention. To boost his social media presence. God, she's nearly as well-known as him around Derry, she doesn't blame him for wanting to show off and clasp onto his 15 minutes of fame. Fair play to him, she thinks, because ultimately hers came at a tragic price. He thanks her, before moving over to the collection of fans clasping posters and CDs, eagerly wanting his attention. Skirting around the feverish teenagers, Cathal nods in the direction of the ex-contestant.

"Making celeb friends?"

Despite the awkward atmosphere between them, Ava gives an honest laugh.

"You know, getting bored around these parts, no-one but our Nadine Coyle to keep me company. Looking to branch out. Sorry, were you looking for a photo of the two of us?" Ava puts her hand behind her head and pouts in mock seduction.

"Naw, I'm sure I can just pull it from your man's Instagram later," he winks at her. "But I will take a quote now, if you don't mind?"

Ava nods as they move over to the side of the pitch for privacy. It's just after 10pm and all that are left are a few stragglers looking for photographs and autographs from the performers, the hospitality crew packing away their things and friends who have obviously experienced an unexpected reunion, as they clutch their irritable kids who aren't at all happy about their parent's conversations. The duo take a seat down at the side, metres from the trees separating the park from the railway tracks, their backs to the city they were campaigning all night for.

"Just say something simple like *I would like to thank everyone for coming and supporting us. You have all been a pivotal movement in our journey towards success.* Then ring me tomorrow when we have gathered up all the money, and I'll let you know how much we've raised," Ava laughs, nodding to Michael as he waves over, making a pantomime of thrusting his thumb behind him towards his rucksack, no doubt filled with all the cash they'd collected tonight.

"That would be perfect. Just in time for publication on Friday."

"No bother."

"Wait, one more thing," he extends his hands before Ava lifts herself up.

Reaching over and grabbing a brown paper bag that Ava hadn't noticed before, he produces two badly battered tinfoil spheres.

"A thanks for treating me to drinks the other night. I didn't know what you liked, so I just asked for it plain. But there's cheese slices and red sauce in here too if you want them?"

Ava undresses the burger and smiles over at him, before requesting the red sauce. With all the stress of the evening she had forgotten to eat dinner.

"Very kind of you, Cathal."

They eat the cold burgers in silence as they survey the dwindling numbers of people. The man stomping on the deflating bouncy castle to squeeze out the last puffs of air. The boy pulling at his mother's arm as he drags her away from her friend, who both hurriedly throw across departing messages and waves. The gaggle of girls still drooling over *The X Factor* star. Three about 14-years-old and a woman with dark spiky hair that Ava guesses is one of their mothers. She can only see her side profile, and it's hard to make out from this far away, but a stab of recognition hits Ava. She squints her eyes in her direction whilst she hears Cathal's voice beside her, but nothing of what he says reaches her ears. She can't take her eyes off the woman. It's the nose, it looks the absolute double of...

"Ava!"

She jumps and her stare is broken. Blinking and looking at the woman again, she realises she has no idea who it is. And she doesn't look familiar whatsoever. Her mind playing tricks on her. Something that happened often in the months after her depression kicked in.

"Sorry, Cathal," she resumes her attention to him. "Thought I saw someone I knew, what were you saying?"

"It looked like you and Darrell Boyle were having quite an intense conversation earlier."

She rolls her eyes, looking down at the remainder of the bun in her hands, the red sauce absorbed into the bap.

"Aye, that man's a dick."

"What all was said?"

She looks at him, her eyebrows raised humorously.

"Off the record?"

"Of course," he pinches his thumb and index finger together, holds them up to his face and follows his lip line, making a corny *'zip'* noise, before revealing that he'd been crossing his fingers on his other hand.

"Naw, I'm wrong. You're the dick," she laughs, punching him lightly on the shoulder.

"No, honestly. I'm all ears and no hidden recording devices."

# Chapter Thirty-Four:

After Ava's caught Cathal up, his face is a mixture of shock and disgust.

"What a dick!"

"Oi, that's what I said."

"What does he think he's going to gain from that? I mean, you could head straight to the press with that. Or his wife. Or his bosses or constituencies. What a sleeze bag."

"I think it was more of a threat," Ava sniffs.

Cathal glances at her with surprise.

"A threat? How?"

"Just the whole *'I underestimated you, you're smarter than you look'* getup that he was doing. I just don't buy into it. I think he was trying to intimidate me."

For a second, Ava thinks about indulging Cathal in the stories of the past week. The shoes. The Letter. The lily. The figures outside her house. But then she stops herself. This boy was a complete stranger until a few days ago. How does she know she can trust him?

"He just means business," she smiles at him. "And I feel like I'm in his way."

Cathal runs off a spiel about how all politicians have too many enemies to count whilst Ava rests her eyes back towards the woman with the dark spiky hair, but she's already climbing the steps, trailing the girls and far too far away to get a closer look. Listening to Cathal, her eyes move left as she takes in the remaining hangover scenes of the night. Squinting at the man putting a deadbolt on the door into his van, she follows him with her eyes as he calls it a night, travelling deeper into the park towards his car.

An emerging figure beneath the canopy of the trees takes her by surprise. She must've physically jolted or exclaimed, because Cathal stops his story and looks over in the same direction as her. The figure sees the two of them and turns and retreats, disappearing once he reaches the mouth of the trees.

"Who was that?" Cathal looks at her perplexed, as Ava stands and fetches her jacket and bag from under her.

"Mark!"

*In Too Deep*

✳✳✳✳

Phil and I took the B&B reservation in Dublin. I drank myself stupid that first night. Trying to drown out the feelings. Trying to drown out the situation. Trying to drown out the foetus growing inside me. Waking with regret as well as sickness in my stomach, I made the decision of going forward with it. If it wasn't shrivelled up and dead inside me. Drenched in every liquor and spirit the bar held. The hangover was a good excuse for why I wouldn't drink the second night. Not yet ready to tell Phil. To tell anyone. I just knew Chris had to be the first. I owed him that much, at least.

I asked him over to the house a few days later. At first, he refused, but I insisted. Saying it was really important. When he arrived, he asked what the point of him coming over was, when we both knew we were done? I remember sitting at the kitchen table, staring at my hands. Him leaning against the sink, talking about how smitten he was at the start. How he fell out of love as fast as he fell into it. Not being able to listen to it any longer, I just spat it out.

"I'm pregnant."

He continued his rant for a few more

seconds before the words settled in. His hand, raised in defiance, falling limp at his side. His mouth agape. It took moments before either of us spoke. We just stared at each other. Gulping sizably, his gaze dropped to the floor.

"Is..." He coughed. "Is it... Mine?"

I slammed my fist on the table, making him jump.

"Of course it's fucking yours!"

"Okay, okay. Sorry."

He sat down opposite me, reaching for my clenched fists. But I saw red. A blinding light.

After the assault was over, I leaned against the back door with tears spilling onto the floor. He continued to sit where he was. Bruises forming on every part of his upper body. He hadn't even tried to stop me. Upon hindsight, I knew why.

I sulked off to bed, crying myself to sleep shortly after hearing him leave without saying a word. I was desperate for a drink.

*In Too Deep*

Bradd Chambers

# Chapter Thirty-Five:

"We made 12,000 nip last night," Michael woops, emerging from the back office where he had been counting their profits.

A gasp of excitement circles the office, Ava realising too late that she didn't react.

"Wow," she blinks and opens her mouth slightly as her colleagues rest their attention on her. "I'm just so shocked. That's far more than I could have expected."

It is true, she isn't lying. But with no sleep the night before, she's finding it hard to keep her spirits up. She had resorted to taking her anti-depressants again. In the depths of the night, when dawn was threatening to break through the clouds, she began to question herself. Her worth. Something she hadn't done in years.

Mark must've taken a short cut through the trees to the carpark, because when she reached it there was no sign of either him or his car. She tried phoning and texting again, but it was fruitless. Deciding against turning up to his house, she had scurried home in a cloud of shame.

Lying in bed with her phone opened at a picture of Mark and her on holidays last year in

Albufeira. She remembered the Chinese tourist staring at her confused as she excitedly requested a picture overlooking the beach. Her thick Derry accent taking him aback. Mark laughing and asking him in a much clearer voice. Their smiles not only prominent, but real. A real smile that hadn't been on her face in days. Not even now.

"That seems an awful lot, Michael," Kat exclaims. "Are you sure? Like... How can we make that much at just one fundraiser?"

"Well... Your man from *The X Factor*'s manager gave us back half of his earnings... And a few of the chippie vans waved away payment," Michael purses his lips.

"But that would still not be near enough," Claire shrugs, biting on the end of her pencil.

"Alright guys, how much did you say we made?" Paddy sings as he wipes his feet on the mat.

Typical Paddy. Always late.

"12,000, Paddy. We're just debating how we made as much."

"Well there was that kid who gave in five grand..."

Everyone in the room turns to Paddy. He looks from one face to the next.

"What?"

"What kid?"

"This wee lad. Came up to me with a brown envelope. Must've been no more than eight. Said this was from his daddy, and pointed in the direction of the stage. Obviously, there were dozens, if not hundreds, of men in that general direction. And he'd ran off towards the bouncy castle by the time I had a chance to look back down towards him. But aye, I had a look inside and it was five bundles of about a grand each."

The team share shocked glances before resting their eyes back on Paddy again.

"Is it legit, like?" Claire narrows her eyes and turns to Michael.

"Aye. I put the UV light through every note," Michael shrugs. "I did see the five bundles, but I just assumed one of you had started counting last night when it had quietened down a little..."

A few of them shake their heads. Ava stares out of the window, chewing her lip, before she realises all eyes are on her.

"Er... Well, that's very nice of them. When Cathal rings I'll make sure to tell him and maybe say we want whoever it is to get in touch with us and we'll do something big for a thanks. That'll attract more attention and, therefore, hopefully more contributions."

"Cathal?" Michael frowns.

"Aye, the journalist from the Letter."

Is she imagining it, or did Michael raise his eyebrows and pout in judgement, before turning towards the kitchen again?

# Chapter Thirty-Six:

Ava's halfway through composing another lengthy apologetic text to Mark when Cathal's name bounces onto her phone screen, her ringtone penetrating the quiet office. She feels herself grow red, deciding to take the call out the back for a slither of privacy. After Michael's look, she's afraid in case the rest judge her for having a personal relationship with Cathal, especially since he's ringing her mobile and not the office. She leaves the door as close to closed as she can without locking herself out before she answers.

"Alright, Ave?"

Another stab of guilt. Only her close family and friends call her that.

"Aye, Cathal, you?"

"All good, all good."

The elephant in the room makes Ava cringe.

"Just out of the court there. Reporting on some petty crime today. Stacks of craic, people forgetting to pay their TV licenses and all. Sorry I couldn't ring sooner."

Ava nods before she realises he can't see her. She's sure there were other reasons.

"Don't worry about it. Took a while for us to count the haul anyway."

"That good, eh?"

"Very good. Over twelve grand to be exact."

Cathal whistles over the phone.

"My tenner seems measly now."

Ava laughs genuinely.

"Don't be silly, of course not. Most people paid a small contribution. It all adds up," she smiles, before coughing and becoming stone faced once again.

Why is she second guessing everything she does with him?

"Funny though," she clears her throat again. "There is a wee favour I need."

"Anything."

"Some kid handed an envelope in, our Paddy thinks there was about five grand in it. We'd love for you to include this in the article to see if we can get whoever his da is to come forward. It'd make it look good."

"You really think a local kid's da handed in that sum of money?"

His tone arouses Ava's suspicion.

"Well... The kid told Paddy that it was from his da, like."

"What age was he?"

"Paddy thinks he was eight or so."

"Kids that age could get it wrong. Maybe there was some sort of fundraiser?"

"A fundraiser for a fundraiser?" she chuckles nervously.

"Weirder things have happened. Maybe it was something the parents did at the side... Or a whip around. I don't know, Ava... I think if someone who could spare five grand to contribute would definitely let everyone know... Don't you?"

Ava blows out, her eyes heavy with exhaustion as she turns to look through the window behind her to the office.

"I can certainly say a large donation was made and if anyone could..."

Ava isn't listening. The phone slips from her hand and falls to the ground with a sharp slap. The hand originally holding it migrating towards her mouth, failing to trap the gasp that escapes and echoes off the walls in the tiny yard. Her back hitting off the gate as she retreats a few steps. Because there, hung up and staring at her, is Mr Ted.

# Chapter Thirty-Seven:

What in under Jesus is he doing here? Swinging from a peg clasped onto a loose wire in her office's back yard? His eyes directed right at her. She hears the faint sound of Cathal's calls from her phone on the ground. Meticulously, she steps over it, crossing the space and snatching Mr Ted from his display. Pushing the door open, she holds him behind her back, glaring into the office and side steps into the kitchen. Her eyes dart around for a place to hide him. There are a handful of cupboards, many used up by cups and bowls. Making a quick decision, she conceals him by shoving him into the cupboard under the sink, the one less used. Behind the bleach and washing up liquid.

Leaning against the work top, she closes her eyes and tries to calm her beating heart. This is definitely a threat. There's no denying this. No one would take her childhood teddy from his home in Robyn's house and leave it strung up in her place of work. Not for innocent reasons. Someone was in Robyn's house. Someone has been outside her house. Someone *has* been following her. Stalking her.

She thinks back on last night. To her altercation with Darrell Boyle. Could he be behind this? Frustrated with her vendetta against him and his party? He wouldn't have to get his hands dirty, after all. A typical politician. She's sure there's dozens, if not hundreds, of people who would happily and eagerly do his behind the scenes work for him. Is that why he was there last night? To keep an eye on her whilst someone broke into Robyn's house? Surely, he'd know that both herself and anyone in her family would be there to support the evening. And Robyn had said herself she was in town all day. Considering the state she was in, Ava's sure she didn't go straight home either. But how would they know Mr Ted was hers? Or the story behind him?

She needs to know. Collecting her phone from the back, she calls out that there's been a problem with Robyn and she'll be back soon, as she thunders through the office, her eyes set on the door. She's had to leave for reasons regarding her aunt numerous times before, but this is the first time she's had to actually lie about it. Never her strong suit, so she keeps her eyes ahead, leaving her colleagues with nothing but the breeze of the door being swung behind her.

# Chapter Thirty-Eight:

There's no answer at Robyn's door. Hammering on it several times, Ava curses before retrieving her keys from her bag. Jostling with the stiff lock, she manages to finally push herself inside. Throwing her bag on the floor beneath the chair in the entryway, thoughts of someone breaking in through the front door forgotten, she quickly steps forward into the hall, calling Robyn's name.

First, she tries the living room. Ignoring the stretch of scenery overlooking the deadly Foyle, she yanks at all the windows, knowing that there isn't much point. They're positioned at the very top of the glass, barely big enough for an arm to fit through. But she needs to be certain. Making her way through to the kitchen, she repeats the harassment on its windows, although they're in similar positions as the living room's. Finally, she gives the back door a good inspection. But there's no signs of any damage and the key is still safely in the drawer where it's always kept.

Uncle Damien was obsessed with keeping the key there, scared that someone could smash the tiny window pane and reach through to let themselves in if it was left in the door. With no signs of intruders, her adrenaline diminishing, she gives the downstairs WC a languid look, knowing full well that not even a hand could fit through that tiny window, which had been painted shut since before she was born.

Climbing the stairs, she shouts her aunt's name once more. Stopping on the landing, she looks into her old bedroom. The empty spot where Mr Ted had sat only days before. Apart from that, the room seems undisturbed.

She finds Robyn in her own bedroom, still asleep. Retching at the stale stench of drink, Ava pulls the curtains and opens the window. But Robyn doesn't stir. Perching down at the end of her bed, Ava stares at her. Or what she can make out of her. Her thick, dark hair encapsulates her face, and she can just make out the glistening of her wedding ring on her hand which is pressed against her eyes.

"Look, Rob. I'm sorry about last night. I am. I just couldn't have anyone drunk at that event. It had to run as smoothly as it could. I'm not saying you would've ruined it, but... For Christ's sake, look at the state of you now. You can't say you weren't absolutely pissed."

Still Robyn doesn't move, short of the rise and fall of the duvet.

"Are you awake?"

Ava leans forward and pulls back the covers. Gasping and jumping back, she sees the inside of the duvet and sheets covered in thick red vomit. Gagging from the smell and the sight, she just about holds down her breakfast as she bends over the side of the bed to retch. Tears uncontrollably collect in her eyes as she opens them when the initial hit subsides. That's when she sees the collection of pills scattered across the carpet, an empty bottle inches from her foot. The prescription with Robyn's name and address imprinted on it. Screaming her name, Ava jolts to her feet and digs around for her phone inside her pocket.

"I need an ambulance. Now!"

# Chapter Thirty-Nine:

Ava finds it hard not to slap Robyn in the face as soon as she sees her smiling up at her from the hospital bed. Instead, she bursts into tears of frustration, sadness and joy. Sinking to her knees, crossing her arms on the bed and letting her head rest on them, she cries and cries. Robyn stroking her hair and attempting to soothe her with soft coos. Reminding her of the early days after her mum's suicide. She'd thought she'd lost her too. And to the same disease.

When Ava comes to grips with herself, she looks up at her aunt. The dark rings under her eyes. The tattered hospital gown. The tube protruding from her nose and around her neck, snaking off to behind the bed. She'd been non-responsive when the ambulance came. They rushed her to Altnagelvin Hospital right away and Ava had paced the corridor for an hour.

A doctor finally came and said she was going to be okay. They'd had to pump her stomach and were keeping her in overnight to keep an eye on her. He'd given Ava a few leaflets on depression and suicide and some organisations who could help her aunt as she tried to ignore the flicker of recognition on the doctor's face.

"Rob... What the fuck?"

"I know," her voice is croaky, and her eyes are still rolling back in her head. "I'm sorry."

"You're sorry!" Ava almost laughs, getting to her feet.

"It wasn't... On purpose," her head lulls back.

Why is she going on like this? Like she's still drunk or high off her meds? Irritation flares in Ava and she tries to extinguish it, knowing it isn't her aunt's fault. Although the doctor said there mightn't be many side effects, she has to remember that Robyn still isn't mentally well. A trauma like this could do God knows what to her.

"What wasn't on purpose, Robyn?"

"I..." Her eyes flicker open and closed. "I forgot... How much I'd taken... Took more... Than I should've... Would never... Do that to you..."

She reaches an arm lazily towards Ava and she takes her hand gratefully. Should she believe her? Looking down at her now, she does. But the hours of those feelings of abandonment resurfacing again are hard to shake off.

They stay like that a while longer until the nurse marches into the room.

"Right, Mrs Friel... We've a bed for you ready upstairs. Can't be lying about here all afternoon, now can we?"

Robyn doesn't respond. She still lies with her eyes closed. Giving Ava flashbacks of a few hours ago. As the nurse kicks at the heels of the legs of Robyn's bed, getting set to wheel her upstairs, she turns to Ava.

"Visiting hours have just finished, I'm afraid. But you can come by and visit later tonight?"

Ava nods as the nurse tells her the ward number, before thanking her and squeezing her aunt's hand one last time. Walking in the opposite direction of the elevators, she gets easily lost in all the corridors that look the same. Finally, seeing the sign for an exit, she turns right and finds herself in A&E. Relatively quiet on a lazy Thursday evening, she walks past the glass windows looking into the waiting room and is surprised to see Mark sitting there.

Whilst waiting for the doctor earlier, Ava had sent him a short text to let him know that Robyn had overdosed and was in hospital. Seeing him now, through the glass, she breaks down as soon as he looks up.

*In Too Deep*

Bradd Chambers

\*\*\*\*

He turned up at my work the next Saturday night. Shortly before closing. I seethed with anger, smiling with clenched teeth as I served the remaining customers. Strutting over, I informed him we were closing in a few moments. Blagging off as if he was a complete stranger. Rachel eyeing us suspiciously. He grabbed my hand as I turned away and asked for me to meet him at Badger's on the corner of Newmarket Street.

I almost didn't go. But Rachel heard the exchange and convinced me to hear him out. Not having a clue that I was almost six weeks pregnant. The bastard didn't move from the bar when I walked in. Didn't even offer me a chair.

"I've been cheating on you."

Although I had an inkling, it didn't help the soaring pain that ripped through my chest. He spoke silently and sullenly. The noise of the packed bar blocking his words from circulating. Our own private party in clear view.

"So, more than once?"

My jaw clenched.

"Aye..."

I guessed from his wording, but a sob still struggled at the back of my throat.

"With that girl. Lindsay?"

He flinched.

"No... Not exactly."

"What the H-" I realised how raised my voice was. Regaining control, I continued. "What do you mean *'not exactly?'*"

"Nothing's happened with us. But it doesn't mean I don't want it to."

I felt like taking his pint glass and smashing it over his head.

"Then who?"

"A few girls. I've been seeing them on and off for a while now."

"How long is a while?"

"Well..." His lips pursed and he stared at the special's sign in thought. "Depends who we're talking about. I mean, the longest is Lisa, I suppose. That's been going on for over a year now."

I nearly dipped to the floor. Nearly fainted. Over a year? How had he been seeing this woman for over a year? And seeing me for months at the same time? And all these other women? I felt sick. I felt like just letting my stomach empty all over the floor.

"I don't want anything to do with this baby," he bit his lip, as if he was telling me that there was no more bread left at the supermarket. "I'm sorry. Children were never in my plan..."

You think this was my plan? I felt like screaming at him. Letting the whole bar of his buddies know what this devious twat had done. But

I wouldn't lower or embarrass myself that way. Instead, I picked up my bag and swung it around my neck. I leaned in close as if to kiss him on the cheek and hissed in his ear.

"Stay the fuck away from me."

Bradd Chambers

# Chapter Forty:

She lies on his sofa with her head in his lap, a moth-eaten blanket covering her.

"I just don't understand why she would want to do something like that."

Mark shuffles uncomfortably beneath her.

"Maybe she did just forget?"

"But enough to knock her unconscious?"

"It was a toxic mix. Lord knows how many different tablets she's on, and how much she drank. You did say she was having wine at lunch. She probably drank all day and night. I wouldn't worry about it too much, Ave. Not until she comes around a bit more and you can speak to her properly.

"To give my honest opinion, I don't think it was intentional. After how your ma's death affected her, and seeing how it affected you... I don't think she'd ever want to bring that to your family's door again... No matter what mental state she's in. I genuinely believe her. The past few times I've seen her she's seemed to get worse and worse. Maybe this is the wake-up call she, or her doctors, need to get her real help."

She snuggles her head closer to his stomach as he consistently rubs his thumb over her arm.

"Well... No matter what, she's lucky to have you, eh? Why did you say you were checking up on her again?"

She jerks bolt upright, her eyes expanding again. With all the chaos, she'd completely forgotten about the earlier events. Guilt batters at her heart as she remembers telling the office that she was checking up on Robyn. Almost like a premonition. Like she'd jinxed it.

"She was just so drunk last night. Wanted to make sure she was okay on my lunch break. Had brought her a bacon bap..."

Ava's glad she's facing away from him. Can't sniff out her lie.

"Well... You're so good for doing so. Otherwise... Who knows?"

He knows better than to continue down that road. Slapping his knees, making Ava jump, he stands and groans, stretching and reaching for her hand.

"C'mon and I'll leave you home."

Mr Ted!

"Er... I need to go to the office and lock up first," she lies. "And my car's at Robyn's. I'll need it for tomorrow. Can you leave me off there?"

He nods, his hand unmoving until she takes it in hers, before he pulls her up onto her feet. Their eyes meet for a split second until he turns and marches out of the living room.

# Chapter Forty-One:

They drive in silence. From Culmore, over the Foyle Bridge and down the Limavady Road until they come to a stop outside Robyn's house. Ava's gaze travels from the passenger side window and into Mark's eyes once more.

"Mark... There's something I have to tell you. Cathal, he's just a-"

"Listen, Ave... Let's not talk about it. Your head will be all over the place right now. And the last thing I want to do is get into a fight. We'll give it a few days. Why don't I come around on Saturday night? We can talk then?"

Brushing her hair out of her eyes, Ava nods reluctantly, squeezing Mark's thigh in his tight suit trousers, before opening the door and exiting his car without another word. Scared in case she'll cry and never stop if she tries to speak again. She knows he's watching her as she climbs the drive. When she comes to a rest beside her car, she hears the hum of the engine bursting to life again and he speeds off. She steals one last glance after him as he goes to turn the corner. Reaching inside her jacket pocket, she blinks. Where are her keys?

After several moments of flailing around searching, she groans. They're in her bag, which she left discarded in Robyn's house. In her frantic rush to get out to the ambulance, she had pulled the door behind her. Reaching the front door, she looks in and sees it sitting where she left it, underneath the seat. Cursing herself, she thinks about ringing Mark to ask him back, but decides against it. The office is only about a 20-minute walk away. The walk will do her the world of good.

# Chapter Forty-Two:

As she reaches the crossroads at the end of the Limavady Road, she waits for the traffic to stop. She stares at the lights, wondering about Mark. About Robyn. About Mr Ted. And finally, about the shoes. The first inclination that something was wrong. Who knew such beautiful shoes could spiral her life out of control? She tries to think back to a time when things were going right for her, even after her mum's death. It seems much longer, but it can't have been more than a few weeks ago at most.

"Hello, hello."

Looking to her right, Ava's shocked to see Cathal making his way down the street towards her.

"Haven't seen you in ages."

She attempts a smile, but she knows it's half-hearted. It seems like everywhere she goes recently, he's there. Is he stalking her? Is he the one behind all of this? After all, all this started when he entered her life.

"What are you doing here?" she tries and fails to keep the suspicion out of her voice.

"Fluff pieces," he nods his head behind him. "Some woman up the road's turning 100. Got a card from the Queen herself," he raises his eyebrows. "No one else in the office is arsed to interview her. So, they sent me."

Ava nods. She's being paranoid. Lack of sleep and her wound up attitude recently isn't helping.

"What happened earlier?"

Ava's eyebrows raise in confusion before she remembers the phone call.

"Aw... To be completely honest, it hasn't been my day."

She can't help but notice Cathal staring between her eyes, knowing full well that she'd been crying.

"Want to talk about it over a drink?"

Ava goes to protest but he waves it away.

"Entirely innocent, I swear. We can even sit on similar sides of the table."

Ava frowns before laughing.

"You know what? A drink sounds great."

# Chapter Forty-Three:

"Well... When you said it wasn't your day, I thought maybe you'd missed the bus or something," Cathal laughs after Ava has filled him in on the recent drama with her aunt.

They're back in their seats beside the toilets in the Icon. The same place they were on Friday night.

"Although, I must admit. I do agree with Mark."

The shock can't be hidden from Ava's face. "You do?"

"Uh... Aye... Ah – Of course, I... Erm..." Cathal starts stammering before sticking out his tongue and taking a sip of his pint. "Sorry... Foreign territory here," he winks.

Ava smiles awkwardly.

"I do agree, aye. I mean, if I ever have kids, I'll never treat them the way my ma or da treated me. So, I don't think your aunt would ever want to bring you the harm that your ma did."

Ava shifts uncomfortably. It's weird to hear someone talk about her mother like this.

"Especially since your aunt knows the pain herself. You learn from your mistakes. Eh?"

Ava nods. She guesses he's right.

"It's just when I moved in with her... She saw how affected I was. And I saw it with her. I just hope it *was* an accidental overdose. There's no way she could be feeling the same as Mum. Although, her husband did leave her quite recently. And I'm sure me moving out didn't really help. I've offered her an in-home carer, but she won't take it. Says she's grand. But... I don't know. I just wish the doctors would hurry up and find out what's wrong with her," she sighs, draining her drink.

She raises the glass and nods her head to Cathal's whilst she swallows, before standing and heading towards the bar. That's when she realises, she has no money. Her notes and card resting in her purse, inside her handbag. She curses and goes back to the table. Luckily, Cathal has read her mind and has a £20 note raised and ready for her.

"No," she sits down, "I'm not taking it."

"It's my turn anyway," he laughs, standing and heading to the bar himself.

When he's returned with their drinks, she thanks him.

"It's not really your turn, you bought the burgers last night," she teases. "And the drinks before these."

He chuckles into his drink.

"I'm sure I can let that slide. They weren't that nice anyway. Had a bit of an icky tummy after mine. Did you feel the same?"

Ava thinks back to her sleepless night of worry. If she did feel unwell because of the burgers, she wouldn't have been able to distinguish between that, the sickly feeling of guilt or the hollow pain in her chest. They drink in silence for a while, before Cathal asks the question Ava always dreads answering.

"So, you say you lived with your aunt after your ma... Passed away. What about your dad?"

Ava takes longer than necessary to put down her glass, swirling the drink around her mouth. Pursing her lips, she rests her eyes on him.

"Snap!"

He looks at her confused.

"You never met your ma. I never met my da."

His eyes glaze over with realisation.

"Oh... I... I'm sorry. Must be the journalist in me."

She shakes her head at his apology.

"You're grand. You didn't know. He left shortly after Mum found out she was pregnant with me. They were only together for a few months. Mum found out he was cheating on her anyway."

Cathal nods along.

"Then he died. Maybe about..." she blows out, one eye half closed in thought. "Five... Six years ago? So, I never got a chance to meet him. Mum just heard from a mutual friend."

"So, he never bothered with you?"

She shakes her head as she takes another sip.

"Nope. Got married to one of those slags he was ridin' behind Mum's back. Had kids with her."

"What a dick. I mean, why stay in their lives and not yours?"

Ava smiles. He's not going to ask a question or make a statement that she hasn't thought of millions of times before.

"Aye… Sure, what can you do? Mum was enough for both parents. She devoted her life to me… I didn't need a da."

Ava thinks back on the months after her mother's death. After Zoe told her the search was being called off. Those Saturdays she would drive back from her part-time job at the City of Derry Airport and take a detour. Park outside and look at the house of her estranged Granny and Grandad, finding it on the funeral director's website. Where everyone came to pay their condolences and grieve her father before he was put to rest in the ground.

So many times she'd wanted to step out of the car and knock on the door. See if *they'd* wanted her. Ask what he was like. See if she had really been better off without him. Scared in case they slammed the door in her face. Or in case they didn't even know about her. Struggling with herself and her thoughts. Wanting that bit of family she'd lost and the bit of family she'd never had.

# Chapter Forty-Four:

"Ava?"

They look up to see Paddy towering over their table. A little tipsy now they're a few drinks in, Ava gasps and totters to her feet. Throwing her arms around him.

"Paddy," she elongates the final letter in his name. "What're you doing here?"

"Just out for dinner with the missus," he points at the bar where Jenny is sitting, waving over towards Ava.

"Oh, lovely."

Paddy eyes Cathal suspiciously.

"Oh, sorry. This is Cathal from the Londonderry Letter."

Cathal nods respectively towards her colleague, who returns the gesture.

"What are you guys doing here? How's your aunt?"

Ava groans at the prospect of re-telling the story again.

"She's in hospital. Accidently overdosed on her pills," Cathal steps in, physically and metaphorically, as he dodges around the table to shake Paddy's hand.

Ava thanks him with a smile.

"Jesus. Is she alright?" Paddy directs the question towards Ava, who has slouched back down into her chair.

"Aye, she's grand. Just monitoring her overnight. Gonna call in later and see her," Ava squints up at him. "There was a whole balls-up between my keys and my car. Was on the way back to the office when I ran into Cathal here," she gestures towards him. "Came in for a drink, and the way my life's going lately I decided I didn't want to stop," she fakes a laugh before sloshing the last of her drink down her throat.

Both Cathal and Paddy raise their eyebrows at her before exchanging looks.

"I'll get her in a taxi soon," Cathal promises.

"Good man," Paddy says. "You might want to get a move on too, Ave. I think visiting time finishes in 20 minutes."

Ava gasps and slugs her head towards her watch. How had she been here for so long? She stands to leave, frantically searching for her bag, before realising it's still stowed away in Robyn's house. Exasperated, she decides she'll have to give the hospital a miss tonight and will just have to be there to collect Robyn first thing in the morning. Twirling around and thanking Cathal for the drinks, she requests the keys to the office off Paddy. He looks at her confused.

"I... Uhh... I have a spare set in my office drawer. For home, I mean. Otherwise I'm on the street tonight," she fakes a laugh.

Seemingly satisfied with her lie, Paddy fights with his keychain to present his set of the office keys.

"While you're in, some guy was ringing looking for you. We suspect it's about the large donation. We said you weren't in but could leave you a message. He got very defensive and curt, saying that it needed to be you, so we gave him your e-mail. Have a look when you get in, we're all dying to know what it's about," he laughs.

Ava nods, thanking them both before staggering towards the door, the keyring looped around her finger so she won't lose or drop it.

# Chapter Forty-Five:

Leering down the hill and around the corner, Ava makes the short distance to the office go much slower due to her drunken state. Spencer Road is quite different in dusk, she observes. No honks of horns as people inch towards the Craigavon Bridge into town. Many of the businesses closed for the day, short of the few bars and restaurants on the street. She almost walks past the door to her office, before giggling to herself, realising her mistake. She decides against turning on the lights as she steps into the office, not wanting to draw any attention to herself.

Locking the door after her, she starts to cross the room. Bumping clumsily into one of the desks, she curses, grabbing her toe. After she's done hopping on one foot, she brings out her phone and turns on the torch app. Meandering around the desks, she creeps into the kitchen. Thankfully, Mr Ted is still safely in his hiding place, undisturbed. She pulls him out and snaps the cupboard door shut. Sneaking out and back into the office, she jumps as her phone starts to ring, echoing throughout the lonely dark office.

"Hello!"

"Everything alright?"

"Aye, Paddy. Jesus, you scared the shite out of me."

She hears him chuckle.

"Wasn't my intention. Did you get a chance to look up your man's e-mail?"

She rolls her eyes to the ceiling and stamps her foot. She just wants to get going.

"I'll have a look now."

Paddy stays silent. Ava widens her eyes and protrudes her lip.

"Hello?"

"Aye, I'm still here. Go on ahead."

Stifling a groan, Ava shakes her computer's mouse to awaken it. Typing in her password, she heads straight for her e-mails. Ten of them unread.

"I take it your man didn't give his name?"

"Nah, was a bit of an odd ball. Which is why we're eager to find out the craic."

Sighing, Ava clicks on the first message, some automated newsletter from another local charity, before tapping the down arrow key, moving through the unopened mail.

"There's nothing here."

"Nothing?"

"Naw," Ava stands, turning her back on the screen and heading to the back door.

"Oh, shame. He might ring back tomorrow?"

"Maybe," Ava nods along, giving the back door a good shove to make sure it's locked, before turning and marching back into the office.

"Awk, I'm raging. We all wanted to know the craic, like. Anyway, Ave. When we're done our dinner, would you like a lift home?"

Ava smiles.

"That would be great, Paddy. Thanks."

Remembering her lie about collecting keys in the office, she'll make sure to ask to be left off at Mark's. If he sees Paddy leaving her off, he'll assume they went for drinks after work. She won't have to lie to him about her tipsy state or company.

"No sweat. We've just finished our starter here so if you give us..."

Ava doesn't hear the rest. Just as she's coming into the office, she sees the shadow of someone pressing their head against the window. Trying and failing to be discreet as the other half of their body hides behind the sign. She stops dead and screams, her phone falling from her hand. The worst thing she could do, because as soon as the sound leaves her mouth, the figure barrels away.

*In Too Deep*

Bradd Chambers

\*\*\*\*

And that was that. I ran into Chris a few times during my pregnancy. Each time getting fatter and uglier. It was like he planned it. Every time I left the house for a quick errand or was rushing to the toilet in Richmond Centre to pee for the fifteenth time that morning... He'd be standing there. Observing. Another girl on his arm. I even saw him with one of the girls I used to go to school with. She blanked me, giving me the impression that she knew, despite the fact we would chat in class.

But every time, he would never look at me. Just stare at the bump. His sprog growing inside me. Kicking at me and making me ill. As if it were cursing me for leaving him. For having my independence and my dignity. I grew to detest the thing. Swearing to myself that I would pawn it off in a children's home as soon as it came out, but never having the balls to actually get something sorted legally.

Then, the due date finally came... And passed. A day late. Two. Three. Seven. Finally, on my ninth day overdue with Satan's love child boiling away inside me, and after the most painful and complicated birth anyone could wish for, I heard little Ava's first cry. And my heart broke. They lay her down beside me and I looked into her beautiful face. How had I hated something so tiny and innocent? I didn't think I'd love anyone as much as I'd loved Chris, but that trumped it. By a mile. Just staring at Baby Ava and listening to her squeals as I soothed her to sleep.

The entire pregnancy, I craved a drink. I was horrible. The anger I'd felt gushing out to anyone who upset or irritated me. I'd secluded myself. Retreated so far into myself that not even Robyn could bring me out of it. It didn't help that Phil moved to Barcelona with his boyfriend to start up a bar business when I only had two months left to go.

But no, as I held Ava in my arms, I decided she was mine. I was keeping her. No-one was ever going to hurt her. To hurt me. I'd stop drinking and devote my life entirely to that little pink bundle. And I did.

*In Too Deep*

Bradd Chambers

# Chapter Forty-Six:

For the second time today, Ava is left speechless whilst someone on the other end of the phone tries to regain her attention. Seemingly giving up, blaming it on a poor connection, Paddy ends the call, whilst Ava continues to stare at the window. Her mouth open, but no more sound coming out. It takes a while before she finally breathes in, her body no longer able to cope from the lack of oxygen. Like not making a sound would erase everything that had just happened.

Eventually snapping out of her trance, Ava finally makes a move. Skirting over to the window, she gazes onto Spencer Road. Everything is quiet. The odd car squealing past. A few lads outside the pub down the street laughing over their smokes. It seems safe enough, she thinks, as she scurries to get the keys on her desk. Stepping out riskily onto the street, she gives it a good look up and down. But nothing looks suspicious. Nothing lurking in the shadows. It has just gotten dark, and the cloudless sky descends down on her, making her shiver in the breeze.

Wrapping her arms around herself, she steps back into her office. Wracking her brain to

remember what the hooded figure looked like...
She comes up short. She never saw a face. Just a
dark figure with hands pressed either side of the
hood. She shivers again at the thought. She thinks
about ringing Mark or Dermott. But what good
could they do? And what would they even say? It
could've been anyone. Someone mistaking the
office for a takeaway or a restaurant. Someone
looking to contribute or volunteer and they arrived
too late. Or someone looking to break in. Someone
harassing and stalking her. Following her here.
Knowing she's alone. Her eyes skirt to the back
yard, looking eerie in the dark. Empty... For now.

She suddenly wants to be far away from
here. But where could she go? She can't ring Mark,
he'd ask why she's drunk. She doesn't want to
admit that she was out for drinks with Cathal. Not
now when they are on speaking terms again. She
can't go home or to Robyn's with no keys. She
thinks of everyone she could phone. Everyone she's
let drop out of her life. Zoe. Dermott. Other friends
from school. Never has she felt so alone yet wanted
to be safe with someone else. Away from prying
eyes. Somewhere where she doesn't have to look in
every corner and constantly over her shoulder to
convince herself she's not being followed.

A thump at the window makes her jump and
scream again. Spinning around, she exhales when
she sees Cathal standing there, waving in at her.
Opening the door for him, she nearly hits him.

"Sorry, didn't mean to startle you."

She knows it isn't his fault. She shouldn't
blame him.

"You okay?"

He observes the dark office.

"Yeah," she throws her jacket over Mr Ted. "Just stuck on where to go."

"Could you not find your spare keys?"

"No. I must've moved them or gave them to someone."

"Who?"

This is why she doesn't lie. She's no good at it.

"I can't remember. Must've been someone like Mark a while back. And he's given them back," she quickly adds as she sees Cathal open his mouth. "Must be in my house somewhere."

Nodding, he leans against Michael's desk. "What about Mark's?"

"I don't think it's a good idea that I land to his after drinking. Especially considering who I've been out with," she's glad it's dark and he can't see her blush.

"Well... We have a spare bedroom, if you'd like?"

Ava goes to protest.

"It's just Orla's old room," he ignores her. "Think it still has princess bedding on it. But it's somewhere to lay your head. Sleep off today and bring in tomorrow. It can't go any worse than today, right?"

The street light outside the window emulates his smile. Ava considers this before nodding. The way the past week or so has been going, she certainly hopes not.

# Chapter Forty-Seven:

"It's not much, but Da bought it outright. So, until we're done for identity fraud, it'll do for now," Cathal laughs as he steps back to let Ava in through the front door.

Ava looks around the bungalow in Glenbrae Gardens, just off the Northland Road and down the hill from where she lived with her mother. A homely house that looks lived in. She can almost feel the memories vibrating off the walls. Something her own house doesn't have. She sometimes feels like a guest in her own home. And not just because it's a rental.

"It's lovely."

Ava steps through to the living room. All the candles and pictures. Brightly coloured décor and thriving plants

"Did you grow up here?"

"Aye, but it didn't look like this back then," Cathal scoffs, throwing himself down on the sofa and resting his feet on the coffee table. "Once I had a bit of money about me, I started buying bits and bobs every pay day. Something to make the place look a bit nicer one step at a time. Take the edge off it."

Ava sits awkwardly on the other sofa. She didn't stop to think that the memories screaming out at her could also be bad ones. She gazes around at the dozens of photographs scattered around the room. Although he seemed irritated that he was a photographer at both charity functions, it's clear that Cathal really does enjoy photographs. She looks between each one, before resting on the one closest to her of a slightly younger looking Cathal and who she can guess is his sister on an older man's knee. There's no denying the family resemblance, it has to be Cathal's dad. With a mop of blonde hair and a copper moustache to match.

The fumes off the candles hit her and she feels herself start to sober up. Is this the best idea? Coming and staying in the house of this man when her boyfriend thinks something is going on between them? Going to an all girl's secondary school, Ava didn't have many friends that were boys. Maybe Mark finds it odd? Or intimidating? Her keeping Cathal a secret surely didn't help. She should've just been open and honest with him from the start and she wouldn't be in this mess.

She counts down from three, telling herself when the countdown is finished that she'll stand and tell him she's going to leave. Take her chances with Mark. But there's a sound in the hall and the living room door is thrust open before she has the chance. Standing there, giving her a look of caution, is a young blonde-haired girl with a scruffy denim jacket. A lot older than the picture, but Ava could still put money on it that it's his sister.

"Alright, Orl?"

"Aye," she says, skirting the walls to keep her distance from Ava. "Who's she?"

"This is my friend, Ava. Say hello."

"Hello, Orla isn't it?"

"I meant Orla say hello," Cathal laughs, biting his nails as he flicks through the TV channels.

"Alright?"

"I'm good, Orla. And you?"

"Are you Cathal's girlfriend?"

"Orla!" Cathal shoots her a look.

"What? I'm just asking. She's the first *girl* you've brought home," she teases, sticking the cords of her hoody in her mouth, before running from the living room.

Ava hears the door in the next room slam.

"Sorry about that," Cathal blushes.

"You're grand," Ava laughs, going to stand.

"Don't let that affect your stay. You have nothing to worry about. I'll talk to her tomorrow," he reassures her.

Ava nods. They continue watching TV for a few moments longer. Ava can't tell whether the silence is awkward or not. If there's tension. And if there is, is she the culprit? Making a drama where there isn't one? Reacting infectiously to Cathal's yawn, she stretches dramatically.

"I might get to bed, y'know? Been one of those days."

"Of course," Cathal climbs to his feet. "I'll show you where to go."

Ava makes for the living room door.

"Don't forget your jacket."

Ava spins around but she's too late. Cathal has grabbed her jacket and is lifting it to pass over when Mr Ted slips from beneath it and falls to the ground. The pair stare at him. Ava scared and Cathal confused. Their eyes finally meet.

"Yours?"

"Aye."

He begins to laugh, bending down to pick him up.

"Big girls don't cry. I won't judge," he winks.

Taking him gratefully, Ava thanks him and turns, trying to hide her face, growing redder by the second. She steps out into the hall and is met with four doors to her left, the front to her right. Maybe she should just go?

"In here," Cathal points to the third room on her left.

Obligatorily, Ava nods and steps through the door. Sure enough, she enters a box room with a single bed plastered in princess bedding. On the wall is a mirror shaped like a fairy tale castle and she nearly trips over a unicorn teddy when she crosses the threshold.

"Sorry about the mess. When my da left, I moved into his room and Orla got my old one. No one's even been in here in months. Only ever gets used if Orla has a mate staying over."

Ava keeps the strained smile on her face and sinks herself onto the bed, which is surprisingly comfortable.

"You need water? Toothpaste? A charger?"

"No, I'm grand. Thanks. Think I just want to go to sleep."

"No bother. Well, if you need me I'm in the bedroom beside ye," he nods his head to the right. "Bathroom's just there," he nods to the adjacent wall. "And if you change your mind and get thirsty or hungry, kitchen's just through the living room. Alright?"

"Never better," she lies.

Smiling down at her, he flicks the side light on and closes the door. Leaving Ava alone in a strange house with nothing but her thoughts.

## Chapter Forty-Eight:

Happy that she's the first in the office, Ava successfully shoves Mr Ted in her desk drawer before Claire battles through the door, the signature half a dozen shopping bags in tow.

"Alright, Claire?" she beams up at her.

"Hiya, Ava," she makes a pantomime of trying not to judge her for wearing yesterday's clothes, but Ava clocks it straight away. "How's your aunt?"

"She's not too bad. Took too many of her prescriptions and ended up being really sick. Had to get her stomach pumped, so they kept her in overnight to make sure she was okay. Going to collect her at lunch time again."

Claire unloads the bags under her desk, talking about how awful that is when Michael scoots through the doors.

"Well, have ya seen we're all famous?" he giggles, shaking the newspaper at them.

"Let's see," Claire shrieks, skipping towards him.

They both meet halfway at Ava's desk, and he spreads the inner page story across her keyboard. The pictures flood back the memories.

There's all five of them standing with their collection buckets and smiling towards the camera, Cathal behind the lens. Sure enough, there's Ava with *The X Factor* star, no doubt plucked from his social media account. Kids having fun on the bouncy castle and playing the games. Ava spots Zoe in the corner of one whilst a girl with a butterfly painted on her face giggles at the thought of getting her picture taken. And at the end of the story, a small segment about the mystery person who donated five grand, and if anyone has any ideas who it is, to come forward.

Of course, none of this is new to Ava. By the time she woke up this morning, Cathal had already gotten two copies.

"Our shop is mobile around here," he winked at her from his coffee cup as she raised an eyebrow at his earliness. "Flies about the place in a wee van. I knew you'd probably want a copy to keep yourself."

She thanked him and sat down to read it, gratefully accepting tea and toast. She'd insisted that he'd done enough for her, but he still forced a tenner into her jacket pocket for a taxi instead of the bus.

"Sure, you'd be terribly late," he laughed, before ruffling Orla's hair and telling her to be good. "And not enough change for that either."

From the taxi, Ava had rung the hospital to check up on Robyn. They'd told her she'd be discharged after midday, and she could pick her up then.

"With what car?" she'd said under her breath as she hung up.

She just hoped that Robyn knew someone that would have a spare key. Otherwise, it was a call to a locksmith and a hefty charge.

"Any word from your man who was ringing yesterday?" Michael asks, bringing Ava back into the present.

"Naw, no word yet."

"He was a while strange one, wasn't he, Claire?"

"Aye. Man on a mission," she giggles into her mug.

Clicking onto Twitter, Ava searches *'@londonderryletter,'* quickly finding the online version of the story and retweeting and liking it. Instantly, she gets a notification that *'@heathermoore71'* has retweeted and liked her retweet. Moments later, she gets a message.

*'@heathermoore71: congrats on your fundraiser!! you did well!!'*

Ava stares at the screen for a few seconds. She wishes this was Facebook or an indirect message where she could just like it and move on. She decides a polite *'thanks :)'* will suffice.

Paddy barrels in ten minutes later with celebratory donuts for everyone.

"Cheers, Paddy," she takes one with pink sprinkles.

"Any luck with the one from yesterday?"

"No," she sings, fighting the urge to roll her eyes.

"Have you checked your e-mails again?"

Ava shakes her head.

"Will check them now."

She finds it four messages down. An e-mail from an *'emmet520DSE@gmail.com.'* She hides the urge to gasp, not wanting to draw attention to herself, as she stares at the line he's sent her. Tears collecting in her eyes.

*'Give me back my money or al snap ur ma's fckin neck.'*

# Chapter Forty-Nine:

Ava blinks. She blinks again. She clicks into another e-mail and then goes back into it. But no matter how many times she stares and whatever she does, the message won't rejiggle into a more comprehensive sentence.

*'Give me back my money or al snap ur ma's fckin neck.'*

She stares at the sender's address. She doesn't know an Emmet. He'd only sent it five minutes ago. After several moments, she clicks the reply button.

*'Emmet,*
*Sorry, I'm confused.*
*Is this the £5,000 that was submitted to the fundraiser the other night that you are referring to?*
*Regards,*
*Ava McFeely,*
*Foundation for Fiona.'*

She re-reads the post several times before clicking send. Leaning back in her chair, she exhales, drumming her fingers on the desktop. A short bleep from the computer's speakers indicates that he's replied instantly.

*'Undeliverable:*

*A communication failure occurred during
the delivery of this message. Please try to resend
the message later.'*

What? Ava resends the e-mail two or three
times but gets the same automatic response. How
can it not send? It's as if the address doesn't exist...

She cups her hands to her mouth, collecting
her thoughts. Does he know her mother is dead?
Not to sound pompous, but not many people
around Derry don't know about her. Is he talking
about the five grand the kid gave in? That's the
only money she could think of. She's taken out no
loans. Hasn't borrowed money from anyone. It's the
only situation she could think of.

"No luck?" Paddy plops a cup of tea down
beside her.

She frantically grabs the mouse and clicks
the *'x'* at the top right-hand corner of her screen,
bringing up her desktop wallpaper.

"No, nothing yet. Must've been a prank call
or something."

Satisfied with her answer, the others go
back to work. Glancing at the time, Ava wishes the
clock to go faster. It's only half nine. She needs an
excuse to get out and clear her head, but she's
already told them that she's collecting Robyn from
the hospital at lunch time. She thinks of someway
she can get out of the office.

Giving up on trying to hide her shaking
hands, she plunges them into her pockets as she
stands and strides into the kitchen. Opening the
fridge, she curses when she sees there's still half a
carton of milk left. No shop runs needed. Closing it

and turning, she looks around for any excuse. Her mind races. Who is this guy? What does he want? Well... Apart from the money? How did this kid get hold of five grand? Is this an all-round threat, or is she targeted specifically? Could this have something to do with Boyle? Should she go to the police?

The police! Dermott! Tugging her phone out of her pocket, she searches Dermott's name and ferociously types out a message asking for him to call her. When the message is sent, she settles back into her chair at her desk for a matter of seconds before her phone rings.

"Excuse me," Ava waves her phone at the guys before turning to the back of the office.

Stopping suddenly, she ponders her actions. She can't go into the back yard without everyone hearing what she says. Turning on her heel, she starts towards the front door.

"Might nip to the shop while I'm taking this, anyone want anything?"

No-one even looks up from their computer. Only when she hears the door click behind her does she answer.

"Hi, Dermott."

"Alright, Ave. You okay?"

"Not really, no."

She's surprised and ashamed to hear her voice crackling and tears collecting in her eyes again. The street is busy.

"Two secs."

She trots across the road and around the corner to behind the businesses, where the quieter streets with the houses are.

"Hi, sorry."

"What's going on?"

Sitting on a pavement behind a navy jeep, Ava bursts into tears and pours her heart out to Dermott.

*In Too Deep*

Bradd Chambers

\*\*\*\*

Of course, being a single mother is hard enough. But being a single mum who is also a recluse with trust issues and a lost respect and hope for men is another. The girls eventually left the shop, and I hired new ones. They were all the same though. Telling me I would meet a man one day to change my way of thinking. Asking me how I went so long without sex. Wondering how my life could just be work and Ava. To be honest, I enjoyed it. It wasn't easy, but it was normal. Respectable. Safe.

As soon as Ava started growing, I knew instantly she would be the spit of her father. She even had his crooked smile. Not when she beamed up at me if she wanted something. But if you caught her off guard. Almost as if she was trying to hide it. And her drive of making the best out of any situation. Her charisma. More things she inherited from him. She never would've got far in life taking after me. And though when we had our stupid mother-daughter spats and all I saw was Chris shouting back, I never resented her. Never questioned *'what if?'* She was the greatest gift I'd ever gotten. The most amazing thing I'd ever created. She was just... Perfect.

Despite my best efforts, I still managed to see Chris the odd time. It didn't matter if I never set foot in his favourite bar or avoided his cul-de-sac, the universe still found a way to push us together. Luckily, I was only with Ava the once. He stared at her and I could swear I saw his eyes fill up. He never tried to make contact. With me or her. Turns out he married the long-term girl, Lisa, and had a bunch of children with her instead. It did hurt, especially after him admitting that children weren't in his plan, but I didn't let it affect me. Affect us.

In the end, I had the last laugh. Because I saw him with other girls as well. His playboy days didn't end there. A wedding ring was easy to slip off. Especially easy to slip off someone's skin as slimy as his. So, when I ever saw him, I held my head up high and strutted past. Showing him what he'd missed. What he could've had. What he lost.

*In Too Deep*

Bradd Chambers

# Chapter Fifty:

Dermott ended up coming over and sitting in a coffee shop with Ava to discuss where she could go from here. He even brought his old colleague, Ethan Bratton, who still works with the PSNI, to take a full statement and make the force aware of the situation. They both warned her that with everything that goes on, in Northern Ireland especially, she'd have to be extra careful. If there *is* someone following her, if they knew that she's went to the police then things could get a hell of a lot worse for her. It purely depends whether it's some sick joke, or if it's gone even further, into the hands of someone high up in a local underground organisation.

"Either way, I think you'll find out soon," Bratton had told her. "I wouldn't go flashing that cash on something pretty for yourself anyway. And don't make yourself predictable. Take different routes to and from work. Stay at different people's houses if you can. Try not to travel at night and stay with company. Anything and everything to keep you safe."

Ava had agreed, thankful that they had both turned up in civvies, before apologising and saying she had to collect her aunt from hospital. Naturally, Dermott wanted to help.

Now, she's sat in his car on the way to the hospital. The short drive is unbearable with the atmosphere in the car. Them both deep in thought. When they reach the hospital, Ava thanks Dermott, who says he'll wait for them in the car park.

The smell hits Ava as soon as she enters. The sickly smell that seems to be reserved for hospitals. Not that it's the smell of the sick people inside, but the overpowering stench of cleaning products. The painted pink walls don't help. Giving her the feeling she's inside a giant stomach.

Ava's just climbing the stairs to Robyn's ward when she sees her bolting out of the double doors into the corridor, slamming the palm of her hand on the elevator call button incessantly.

"Mrs Friel, we need you to stay until someone's ready to collect you," a nurse pleads with her.

"I'm checking myself out, by fuck am I staying here," Robyn grunts, her head lifted towards the number above the elevator doors.

It's still a few floors away.

"Everything okay?"

Hearing Ava's voice, it's like a switch goes off inside Robyn. Her harsh demeanour diminishes and she turns and collapses into her arms.

"Get me home. Please, just get me home."

"What's wrong, Rob?"

"They're trying to pump me full of God knows what. I just want my own bed. It's been a rough night. Bastards wake you up every time you try and sleep to ask you if you're sleeping. My blood pressure taken every half a fuckin' hour. I want out," she stamps her bare foot on the floor.

"That's fine, Mrs Friel," the nurse tries to soothe her again. "The doctor's gonna be right with you. He'll be able to discharge you and we can get all your stuff and your daughter here can take you home," she nods at Ava who smiles at her, not bothering to correct her in case Robyn kicks off again.

"C'mon, Rob. Let the doctor see you one last time to make sure you're fit–"

"I know I'm fit to go home!"

"And I know that too. But it saves you coming back in for check-ups and that kind of thing," she feels and sounds like she's talking to a toddler. "Prove to the doctors that you're okay, and we can get away and get some lunch. Okay?"

Mumbling incomprehensibly, Robyn allows herself to be led back into the ward.

# Chapter Fifty-One:

Waiting for the doctor, Ava helps Robyn back into the, rather sodden, clothes that she was wearing when she found her. When she's dressed and ready to go, she helps Robyn into the chair whilst Ava rests on the bed.

"So... Do you really feel better?"

Robyn's eyes sparkle as she smiles up at her.

"Of course, love. Sorry to give you a fright. I know what must've been going through your head. But no, I'm not leaving anytime soon. Not intentionally anyway," she goes to laugh before she stops herself, given the reality of the situation.

"I really hope so, Rob. Are they cutting down your meds?"

She blows a raspberry.

"Think they're heaping a few more into me."

Ava shakes her head, staring at her wide eyed, going to say something before a nurse comes in with a cart displaying several bowls of, rather unpleasant smelling, stew and tubs of plain yoghurt.

"None for me, thanks. I'm on my way home," Robyn smiles at her.

That reminds Ava.

"Have you given anyone a spare key to your house?"

Robyn gives her a peculiar look.

"Heavens no. Why?"

Groaning, Ava leans back on the bed, using her elbows to keep her propped up whilst her feet dangle off the edge.

"Looks like we're going to have to call a locksmith."

"Whatever for?"

"'Cause I left in such a rush with you and the ambulance that I forgot my bag in your house. Unless you happen to have keys on your person right now?"

Robyn shakes her head, giving herself a good pat down just in case.

"I'll give Damien a ring."

Robyn gasps like she's watching one of her soaps.

"You'll do no such thing."

Ava stares at her, confused by her reaction.

"Rob, he'd want to know about this. Even if he doesn't want to help, he can still lend us his key."

"You're not disturbing him. Christ, he *left* me. Last thing he needs to do is gloat that he was right. No, I have a spare key in the back garden. I'll dig it out when we get there."

"What do you mean '*gloat that he was right?*'"

Robyn goes to speak before stopping herself. She shoots a glance at the door and, sure enough, in comes the doctor. He stops with the

249

lady closest to the door first, overlooking her charts hanging at the bottom of her bed. He gives Robyn plenty of time to answer the question, but Ava doesn't press her. The way she's been going on recently, Ava doesn't want to be the one to push her over the edge completely.

# Chapter Fifty-Two:

Helping Robyn out of his front passenger seat and up the drive, Dermott skirts around Ava's car and towards the back of her house. The back gate opens with a squeak, Ava stepping through to the immaculately kept garden. Despite the mess in Robyn's mind and life, she'd never let her garden grow wild and untamed.

"It's just over there underneath the wee gnome with the blue hat," Robyn sighs, the uphill climb taking it out of her, despite leaning on Dermott for the majority of it.

Ava reaches the three gnomes at the corner of the garden. She remembers being banned from playing with them when she was a kid in case she accidently smashed them. She bends down to pick up the smaller one with the blue slouched hat. Raging with herself, and with Robyn, for not giving her this information previously. Could've saved herself a whole lot of hassle. Another sinister thought crosses her mind that maybe this is how Mr Ted came to be in her possession? But when she lifts the gnome, there's nothing underneath. Raising its bottom to face her, she doesn't see a key there, either. Reaching and lifting the other two larger ones, she finds the same result.

"Oh, come on, Ava. I'm dying for a cup of tea and a sit down."

"There isn't a key here, Rob."

"Awk, there is. The one with the blue hat. Right under him."

"I'm telling you, there isn't," Ava stands and brandishes the gnome in her direction. "See?"

"Now, that can't be right," she hobbles over, looking at the space where the gnome once was, before alternating her attention between there and the gnome in Ava's hand. "It's always been kept there."

They spend several moments searching around the garden for the key, coming up unsuccessful.

"When's the last time you actually saw the key, Robyn?" Dermott asks as he pushes the black bin back into place.

She purses her lips and stares in through her kitchen window.

"God... Years and years ago."

"And no-one ever knew it was there?" Ava stands, wiping muck from her hands onto her jeans.

"Nope, just me. Now can you open the door to we get a nice cup of tea?"

She registers the back door whilst Ava and Dermott exchange glances.

"I know a guy," Dermott brings out his phone. "Could be here in a half hour flat."

"Thanks, Dermott," Ava squeezes his arm in affection. "And, sorry about her. Her head's away."

Dermott laughs off her apology, before crossing the grass to tell Robyn he's going to ring his mate. Whilst they're busy disputing, Ava sneaks out to beside her car, loading Damien's number on her phone. Pressing the ring button, she holds the phone up to her ear.

*'The person you are calling is unable to take your call. Please leave a message after the tone.'*

Bringing the phone away from her ear, she clicks into their shared text messages. It's been a few months, but it's definitely the right number. Trying again, she gets infuriated by the same automated response. What has happened between Damien and Robyn?

# Chapter Fifty-Three:

A little over an hour later, they're finally inside the house. The locksmith is just about to leave after a cup of tea and a promise of a bill through the door, since he's doing his good friend Dermott a favour, when he stops at the back door.

"Damien Friel?"

All three of their heads shoot up from the kitchen table. But he's looking at a picture on the wooden unit. One taken a few years back of Damien and Robyn at a friend's wedding.

"Aye, do you know him?" Ava stands and skirts around the table to beside where he's stopped.

"I do surely. Used to work jobs for and with him all the time," he turns to Robyn. "You his wife?"

Robyn bites her lip.

"Erm... Aye, I suppose."

"You suppose?"

The four fall silent.

"Anyway," he doesn't dillydally or pry any further. "Let him know I was asking about him. Haven't heard or saw head nor tail of him in months. Must be a busy man. Right you are."

And with that, he bows down and leaves through the back door. Robyn sits stirring her untouched cup of tea whilst Dermott and Ava share another glance.

"I best be off too," Dermott slaps his knees as he stands, making Robyn flinch. "Hope you're feeling better, Robyn. Make sure and get plenty of rest. Will do you good."

She nods and thanks him. Still not taking her eyes off the tea. He raises his eyebrows at Ava, who leads him out to the front door.

"Thanks so much for all of this, you really are a lifesaver," Ava smiles up at him, even as he turns at the bottom step down to the drive.

"Don't mention it, darlin'. And…" He looks around him before leaning in close. "Don't worry about all that carry on. Bratton's the best in the business for getting stuff done. I'll have money on it that he's fast-tracking everything through as we speak."

Ava looks at her feet before nodding, feeling as useless as Robyn. He taps her shoulder reassuringly, before crunching down the drive. She waves him off, closing the door and going back in to check on her aunt. She's still in the same position as they left her.

"You alright, Robyn?"

She nods again.

"Maybe you should get to your bed?"

Still she nods whilst standing, letting Ava lead her up the stairs. Forgetting the bed sheets are still covered in sick, she puts her down in Ava's old bedroom. Pulling the blankets right up to her chin, she's halfway out the door when she hears Robyn mumbling.

"You say something?"

"I'm sorry."

"Sorry for what, Robyn?"

Seconds pass by, Ava staring at the back of her head as she faces the wall.

"Why are you sorry?"

"When the nurse called you my daughter. You didn't object. And neither did I. I never would. You always were the closest thing to a daughter to me, Ava."

Ava smiles away her embarrassment.

"Sure, what's that to apologise about?"

Robyn begins snoring lightly. Ava closes the door tight and goes to make a start on stripping the bed.

# Chapter Fifty-Four:

When there are fresh sheets on the bed and the dirty ones in the washing machine, Ava looks in on Robyn again. She still hasn't moved. She'll leave her there a while. No point in moving her. Picking up all the pills and chucking them in the bin, she thinks it's best if she stays here tonight. Just to keep an eye on her. And what Bratton said spooked her a little.

Glancing at the clock, she sees it's coming up to 3pm. She'll show her face for two hours in work, before the weekend where she can finally get her head straight. She's not been back since she told them she was going to the shop. She needs to show them she's in control of some part of her life, even though right now it seems like all the plates are no longer spinning, but smashed on the ground.

Sneaking down the stairs, Ava goes to bend down to retrieve her bag from under the chair in the entryway, but it's not there. Instead, it's sitting on top of the chair, plumped against the flowery cushion. Ava stops and stares at it confused. She's nearly sure she threw it under the chair. Didn't she give it a kick for good measure? Did she move it when she came back in earlier, when she thought she had to pay the locksmith? Maybe he moved it? Or Dermott moved it? Or even Robyn? She shakes her head as she pulls the straps up onto her shoulder. She's losing her mind. Must be something in the air, she thinks, as she soundlessly closes the front door behind her.

*In Too Deep*

\*\*\*\*

Ava asked about him shortly after her eighth birthday. I was surprised that it took her so long. When she was very young and confused, she called Damien '*Da-Da*,' despite us correcting her countless amount of times. But that was the only times the subject was broached until then. Obviously, I saw her looking at other girls with their dads on the street or in the park, and always managed to cast a glimpse her way if something relatable came up on TV. But she never mentioned it. Not until that night.

I put it down to me being enough for her. Everything for her. Like I tried to be. I was the breadwinner and both parents. The best friend. The nurse. Santa. I had no time for socialising or dating or drinking. The odd dinner with Robyn and Damien was all I could muster, and even then, Ava came too. But I should've known that the questions would eventually come.

It was a lazy Sunday night in front of *Friends* when the moment arose. I tried to be sympathetic but blunt with her. I never lied, and I didn't relay information that she didn't intentionally ask for.

Over the next few years, she would understand the greater picture through moments similar to that one. She respected that I was hurt and never probed further than she knew she could. She was patient and sweet, just like she was with everything else in life. Something she didn't get from him, I was happy to recognise. She had inherited most of my good traits. It was just the odd infuriatingly bad one that descended from him, like a shadow crossing over her face.

*In Too Deep*

Bradd Chambers

# Chapter Fifty-Five:

Pulling up the handbrake as she parks in her drive after work, Ava takes a moment just for herself. She had gone such an arse about face way of getting home. Firstly, she went over the Craigavon Bridge on the upper deck, before swinging around the roundabout and travelling back over the bottom. When she reached the Limavady Road, she turned left and went over the Foyle Bridge, then went right over the border to get petrol. Swung in to Culmore on the way home and drove around Mark's estate, before pulling out on a country road and driving straight until she got to Ballyarnett. She took a detour around Galliagh, before finally arriving home.

And for what? To go inside and collect a few things before doing the whole roundabout drive back to Robyn's? She kept one eye on her rear-view mirror the whole time. Luckily, she didn't feel like anyone was following her, although she *was* overly suspicious of everyone. Slowing down to see if they'd attempt to overtake her or indicating to see if they'd copy her.

Stepping out of the car and pulling open the back door, Mr Ted safely disguised within her jacket once more, she starts up her drive. When safely inside, she gazes around at the home she's made for herself. The cheap IKEA furniture. The fake plants protruding out of their vases. Everything pristine and polished, like a show house. Unlived in.

It certainly feels unlived in, she thinks, as she trots up the stairs. It's only been about 36 hours since she was last here, but so much has changed and happened since then that it feels like it's been a lifetime. And she can't help but compare the feel of it to Cathal's house. In contrast to his, hers feels cold. Unloved.

She pledges that once she has things sorted out with Mark, they'll properly move forward. They've been together three years and they're not getting any younger. He certainly isn't, she thinks jokingly. He'd hinted on moving in together in the past, and she'd panicked. Afraid to let herself get close to someone again. Now, with his absence, she feels like it's the right time. Maybe it's what she needed to make her realise how much she misses him and what he means to her?

She puts Mr Ted down delicately on her bed, propped against a pillow. As she throws bundles of clothes and toiletries into a suitcase, she stops suddenly when she sees an unfamiliar car outside. Parked right opposite her house. A shiny black BMW. She whistles as she admires it, until, seconds later, it revs its engine and speeds out of sight. Confused, Ava hopes that it wasn't watching her house. Or didn't have someone getting out of it. Slowly making their way up her drive to her front door...

Her phone ringing makes her jolt out of her daydream. Is it a daydream if it's scary? Or would you call it a daymare? She's unsure. A withheld number, she observes as she glances at her screen. Now she really does feel herself start to panic. Clearing her throat, she lifts it to her ear.

"Hello?"

"Ava, Ethan Bratton here."

She lets out a sigh of relief.

"Phew, I'm glad it's you. You had me worried there."

"You won't be glad for very much longer, I'm afraid."

She tenses.

"Okay..."

"We had a look at that e-mail address. It was created and accessed today shortly after 9am. Just long enough to send you that e-mail, then they went offline. Been deactivated. They haven't been on since, but we have people monitoring it. However, it's the place that's the problem."

Ava's interruption on IP addresses and the likes is quickly dismissed, without even presenting it.

"It was created, and the actual e-mail was sent, from inside Lisnagelvin Shopping Centre."

Ava nods, finding herself deflating. Lisnagelvin Shopping Centre is very popular in the Waterside of the city due to its amenities, including a 24-hour Tesco, butchers, several health and beauty shops and cafés. Absolutely anybody could've sent that e-mail.

"We're currently looking into CCTV from the centre, but I'm sure you know where I'm going with this."

Ava tells Bratton that she understands as she pulls the suitcase down the stairs, several garments of clothing still protruding out of the hastily zipped corners. Remembering the shepherd's pie in the fridge, Ava leaves the case in the hallway before crossing into the kitchen to retrieve it.

"Sure, you tried your best and that's all that matters. Thanks, I'm just about to leave and stay at my aunt's for the evening anyway."

"Good. Stay safe and we'll keep you updated if there's any progress."

Thanking him again, Ava hangs up. Reaching into the fridge, she retrieves her dinner before turning back towards the door. That's when something catches her eye on the kitchen table. Shifting over, she sees it's the photograph Robyn gave her the other day. Only she didn't leave it on the kitchen table. She didn't even take it out of her bag. And, if that wasn't enough, it's been altered. Now, instead of Robyn smiling up at her, there's a massive *'x'* etched over her face in thick red marker.

# Chapter Fifty-Six:

Crashing through the front door and thundering up the stairs, Ava gasps when she sees the crumpled sheets in her old bedroom. Robyn nowhere to be seen.

"Robyn!" She screams, running into the master bedroom, but it's exactly how she left it.

She shouts her name a few more times, looking in the bathroom and even chancing her arm with the hot press, before taking the stairs two at a time, only to come face to face with her aunt as she hits the bottom.

"What's wrong, love?" Robyn's voice is muffled as Ava pulls her in for a hug.

Feelings of relief over, Ava pulls away and holds her by the shoulders.

"Listen. Are you 100% sure that there was a key in the garden?"

"Aye, why would I-"

"No, Rob. I'm serious, you have to be honest with me. Does *anyone* know about that spare key? Friends? Neighbours? Damien?"

Robyn bursts into laughter when Ava mentions the latter.

"Damien? He'd have me strung up if he knew that I had a spare key outside. Always thought we were going to be broken into, didn't he?"

Ava battles with herself to not indulge the irony of Robyn's statement as she stares into her eyes. A little sleepy, but you can tell she hasn't had a drink, and doesn't look as badly affected by the medication as she sometimes does. She thinks she can trust her.

"When did you put it out there?"

"Like I said, years and years ago," Robyn pulls away and reverts back into the kitchen. "After Damien got that new door put in, I kept forgetting my key. Had to wait until he'd come home from work to get back in. It happened three times in one week before I decided, to Hell with it. I'd get a spare done behind his back. Only used it a handful of times 'cause by the time I'd went into town to get the key cut, I'd got used to the door," she giggles, plopping tea bags in a mug. "I don't know how I'm ever gonna sleep tonight now after that nap."

"Look, Robyn. We have to go."

"But, why?"

Ava looks around the room. Trying to think of a way out of this mess without telling Robyn the truth. It'd imbalance her mood and God knows what could happen. She might be uncooperative.

"We've just had such a stressful few days. I thought we should go out to eat."

"No thanks, love. I'd rather get a Chinese and catch up with my programmes."

Cursing to herself, Ava turns her back on her aunt. Desperately thinking of something to get her out of the house. That's when she sees the gift vouchers for the Shandon Hotel and Spa in Donegal that she'd gotten Robyn last Christmas.

"Look, Rob. I didn't want to tell you this," she skirts over and pockets the vouchers discreetly. "But I've booked for us to go away for the night. I wanted it to be a surprise, but you're making it much harder than I'd thought."

Robyn exclaims dramatically, pressing her hands to her cheeks.

"Oh, Ave. Really? Why ever for?"

"Like I said... It's been a hard few days," she looks away like she's getting emotional, knowing it'll hook her aunt right in.

"Oh, pet. Thank you so much. Right, I'll go start to pack. What should I be bringing?"

"Just throw in anything. It's a bit of a drive so be quick."

Robyn rushes over and smacks a sloppy kiss on Ava's head.

"And a swimsuit," Ava shouts after her as Robyn climbs the stairs excitedly.

When she's safely out of ear shot, Ava brings out her phone.

"Jesus, Ava. I've heard from you more the past week than I've done in months," belly laughs Dermott as he answers on the third ring.

"I know, I know. I'm so sorry. But here, I need another *massive* favour."

"Anything, love."

"I swung by my house to collect my things after work, before coming back to sleep at Robyn's. There's a picture that was in my handbag, which was obviously locked in Robyn's, which I think was definitely moved because I left it under the chair, but it wasn't under the chair. But anyway, the picture has a huge red 'x' over Robyn's face. It's a threat. And he stole it from my handbag, and he must've got hold of my keys to let himself into my house, although I don't understand why he put my keys back and not Robyn's. But now I know he has Robyn's spare key and he'll come back. So, I nee-"

"Wow, wow, wow, girl. Take a breath. Calm down, one step at a time."

Ava inhales, realising she wasn't talking sense.

"What is it you need from me?"

"I'm taking Robyn away now overnight. I need you to call your locksmith mate and get brand new locks put into both of Robyn's doors. And my own as well, actually. In case he's made spares. Whoever is harassing us has that missing spare key of Robyn's. I just know it. I don't know how he knew it was there, but he's got it. And I'm really afraid for her safety."

"Okay. I'm not really sure what's going on, but okay. I can be there in twenty minutes?"

"Maybe make it a half hour so we're definitely gone. Thanks, Dermott. I'll leave the keys out for you to get in with your man."

"But where are you going to leave them?"

Despite the horrific situation that they're in, Ava still manages to laugh.

# Chapter Fifty-Seven:

"Awk, Ava. It's lovely."

It buckin' better be, she thinks, as she hauls the cases into the room. Even with the voucher, it had still cost her an arm and a leg for the room. The receptionist reassuring her that this was the only one of three left, so they were lucky. She didn't feel lucky as she punched her pin into the machine.

After a quick stop at hers, to pick up her swimming costume, they had hit the country roads through Donegal to the Shandon, situated just outside Portnablagh and overlooking the beach at the bottom of Marble Hill. She stares down at it now from the hotel window as dusk settles. They're too late for any spa treatments, so until tomorrow they'd have to make do with dinner and drinks at the bar.

Turning and admiring the room, she's unsurprised to see Robyn pouring out a glass of wine from the bottle she'd brought with her.

"Want one?" she offers her the glass she'd just filled.

"Aye, why not?" Ava thanks her, before downing half the glass in one.

"Wait 'til I catch up, God's sakes," her aunt tuts, rushing to fill her glass.

Lounging on the bed, Ava remembers coming here with Mark. Their antics in the hot tub and underneath the sheets. It was their first anniversary, but was close to coming up to a year since her mother's death. She cried herself to sleep in his arms when she'd had a few too many cocktails and had started to reminisce. They'd survived all of that, she thinks, they're bound to survive this tiny hiccup.

"Right, I don't know about you, but I'm starving. Barely ate anything in that hospital. Why don't we go and see what the food's like?" Robyn says, sliding off her slippers and into a sparkly pair of flip-flops.

Ava beams up at her, deciding to forget about the troubles of the past few days and enjoy her night with Rob, who seems in great spirits.

"No bother, I already know I'm getting the chicken. It was lovely last time."

# Chapter Fifty-Eight:

It's way past closing time when Ava and Robyn finally fall out of the bar into the corridor, forcing a rather impatient and tired looking barman to fail to hide a smile as he closes the door behind them. They roll around the floor laughing for a while, holding onto each other. They had drunk *a lot*. This is the drunkest Ava has been since she was a teenager. Robyn just kept refilling her glass.

"Here, I've an idea," Robyn struggles to her feet, holding out a hand to pull Ava up along with her. "Let's go to the beach."

For some reason, the idea is hilarious. They race each other down to reception and out of the door, panting down the drive until they come out onto the lane. Discarding their shoes at the top of the steps, they hop down them and onto the beach, the sand slowing them down, sucking them under as they desperately try to fight their way to the sea. Only when they're ankle deep in the cold water do they stop.

Holding onto each other, still laughing while gasping for breath, they look out onto the vista. The moon is full and bright as they survey the beach. The night air tepid to stop them shivering.

When they finally catch their breath, the water sobering them slightly, they migrate up the beach and plonk themselves down on fluffy sand, metres from the waves.

"It's so beautiful down here," Ava observes, running a hand through her hair, knowing she'll be picking sand out of it all tomorrow morning but no longer caring.

She knows she should be looking out to make sure no one's watching her. Coming up behind her. But she doesn't care about that either. She'd taken many winding roads, dodgy pull-outs in traffic and ran a few too many red lights to make sure they weren't being followed here. She loses herself for a few moments. Pressing down her fear. Daring something to happen. The serenity of the night floods through her. It's perfect.

"Your mum loved the beach," Robyn stares straight in front, right out into the sea.

Ava looks at her desperately. Robyn hardly ever mentions her sister, and if the subject is breached, she quickly changes it.

"Used to love collecting shells. I remember saving up and buying her a plain wooden jewellery box for her birthday one year. She fell in love with it, like I knew she would. We spent all day gluing the shells onto it, and the ones we had left over we stored inside it. She kept it on her bedside table for a long, long time.

"We had a massive row a few years later, and I smashed that same jewellery box against the wall. God, did we fight growing up. Her wanting to be old before her time, me still wishing I was as young as her."

There was an impressive 12-year-gap between Robyn and Ava's mum. She used to joke that she was the *'oops'* baby, as her parents had been defiant that they would only have one child, Robyn.

"She was always so mature, so driven... I have no idea where she got it from," she laughs, choking up. "Probably Mum and Dad. They saw themselves in her."

Ava watches her aunt as she, understandably, remembers her dead parents. Her dead sister. Her eyes glazed over with memories and tears. Putting an arm around her, Ava presses her head into her shoulder. They sit for a while longer before Ava finally spits the request out.

"Tell me about that night again."

Robyn stiffens.

"You don't want to hear that."

"I do."

"Once was enough."

"You told it to the police countless times," Ava pulls away from her embrace.

"And every time it hurt less and less until it numbed me. I don't want the same thing to happen to you."

"It won't, I promise. I just want to... Remember her."

Robyn stares at her for a while before finally nodding her head, tapping her knee for Ava to lay her head down properly. They lie and listen to the waves crashing, sinking into the sand, while Robyn thinks about where to start.

"She texted me to tell me she couldn't do it anymore. That she needed to go. I always knew she had problems. Problems she kept hidden from you for your own sake. She said she loved me, and she loved you, but we were better off without her. Told me she was leaving all her possessions to you for when you turned 18, and for me to make sure that you got them.

"I just instantly knew what she was doing. I jumped in the car and sped towards the bridge, finding her about halfway over. One leg on either side of the railings. I got out of the car and sprinted towards her, shouting for her to stop. She looked up at me and I could see she was crying. She told me to look after you... And then... She did it. She just slid right off."

Both of them are crying freely now, clinging onto each other for entirely different support than a half hour ago.

"I ran over to the railings, but she was already gone. I rang the police and they got in contact with the Foyle Search and Rescue. They patrolled that river for hours, and I sat in the back of a police car with a stupid tinfoil blanket wrapped around me. Feeling completely useless. Just hoping and praying that they'd find her alive. That they'd drag her out of that awful river... But they never did."

*In Too Deep*

Bradd Chambers

\*\*\*\*

And then Chris died. Just like that, he was gone. Not that he was ever present. But I still saw him a few times a year. And knew where I could find him on any given Friday or Saturday night. I never spoke to him, of course. But it's just odd that someone that once meant so much to me, and helped procreate the most special person in my life, was just... No longer there.

Robyn told me. A girl in her work who was friends with Lisa on Facebook had seen it. I spent all day wondering whether to tell Ava. Why should she care? Would she want to go to the funeral? Make amends with the family? With her half brothers and sisters? I didn't want that. What if they didn't know about her? If they were never told? What kind of can of worms would that have released into our lives? And theirs? But I couldn't be selfish. Ava had to make her own decision. This was the only chance she would ever get.

I told her after school that day. I collected her and we walked through Brooke Park as it was a nice enough day. Her expression changed when I told her the news. She was more confused than upset. She asked me what she should do.

Everything screamed at me to tell her to run from it. Forget about it. Good riddance. But I couldn't. I told her it was her decision.

She agreed to go to the funeral. She didn't have anything black, so we went to Next to get her a dress and a cardigan. When I went up to pay, she said she felt sick. Running out of the shop, she stood overlooking the railings in Foyleside Shopping Centre. I really thought she'd vomited over the side. Thankfully, she hadn't. I took her hand and walked her home, before nuzzling onto the sofa with her. Her favourite soup boiling on the stove and her reign over the remote control.

She didn't go in the end. We were all set and ready, me walking her there, obviously. Damien ready to go and sit in the church with her. But once she came down the stairs, I knew she wasn't going. She was pale white, no colour in her face. The black on black didn't help. She always wore colourful garments. She stopped a few steps from the bottom and shook her head. We asked her if she'd regret it. If she wanted to go and stay in her car. Watch the burial from afar. She didn't say anything, just shook her head once more, before turning and marching straight back up the stairs again. My stubbornness shining through with every ascended step.

*In Too Deep*

Bradd Chambers

# Chapter Fifty-Nine:

She wakes with her tongue stuck to the roof of her mouth. Reaching out blindly to the bedside table, she fails to grab hold of any form of liquid. Squinting one eye open, it takes her a while to realise where she is. She twists around and sees Robyn snoozing beside her. Still no sign of water anywhere. She tears her lips apart painfully, remembering the bottle of Diet Coke in her bag.

Sipping on the warm flat liquid, she thinks back on last night. She doesn't even remember leaving the beach or getting back into the hotel, never mind to bed. Resting on the seat by the window, she looks out onto the dreary day, her eyes settling on the beach. Remembering everything that was said.

She'd heard it all before, of course. Three years ago. At her mum's memorial service. Robyn crying outside the chapel, confessing to her what had happened. Tight lipped for weeks before. She was scared in case Ava would blame her. Ava had told her she was being ridiculous.

Bringing her phone out of her bag, she switches it on. As soon as she crossed the border, she had got attacked with text messages and e-

mails about different deals and tariffs, so she'd
turned it off to give herself a bit of peace. Switching
it to silent mode in fear of waking her aunt, she
sends Dermott a quick text asking for progress. She
doesn't expect him to text back first thing on a
Saturday morning, but he does.

*'Only managed to get Robyn's done last
night. Over at yours this morning. I'll leave both
keys in our safe place. D x.'*

Ava throws him a quick thanks as she hears
Robyn stirring. Switching her phone off again, she
waltzes over and sits at the foot of the bed. Ava
smiles down at Robyn as she looks up, bleary eyed,
her cropped hair dishevelled.

"Alright, love?"

"Aye, you?"

"Apart from my mouth feeling like a fur
boot?"

Ava snorts as she hands Robyn the residual
Coke.

"I had fun last night," Ava blushes as her
aunt drains the bottle.

"Me too, we should do it more often,"
Robyn smiles. "But, the fun's not over yet. Let's get
ready for our fabulous spa day, darling," she puts
on a posh English accent that leaves Ava cackling.

# Chapter Sixty:

The pair laugh and share stories the whole drive home. After an immense breakfast, the day was spent lounging around in dressing gowns and a full body massage that was so relaxing it almost made Ava forget about the trouble of the past few days.

When they pull into Derry City, Ava remembers about the new key and starts panicking. Thinking of different ways she can present the story of getting brand new keys cut without Robyn speculating that anything sinister is going on.

"I had a lovely night and day," Robyn squeezes Ava's hand as it rests on the gearstick. "Why don't I treat you to dinner?"

Ava's smile breaks out and she nods. Forgetting to act noble, trying not to arouse suspicion, she half attempts denial, but thankfully, Robyn insists. She parks by the quay, the river separating them from Robyn's house. Robyn goes to get out whilst Ava fights with her handbag, finally finding her phone.

"Er... Go and grab us a table, will you? I need to make a quick phone call. Business," she adds as Robyn gives her an odd look.

Shrugging her shoulders, she makes a start across the road whilst Ava turns on her phone. She's bombarded with text message tones, but she ignores them as she rings Dermott's number.

"Alright, stranger?"

"Not so bad, Dermott. You're not going to believe this, but I need one last favour. I haven't told Robyn anything that's been going on. I'm too afraid it'll upset her and set off one of her moods. And after the past few days, I'm scared of what she'll do. She's taking me out for dinner here, is there any chance you could meet us at her house? Pretend you're just calling around to check up on her, like? And pass me the key? Then I'll change her key for the new one whilst you distract her. I know I've been asking a whole lot of you recently, I owe you about twelve pints. But this is the last one, I promise."

"Don't make promises you can't keep. And don't worry about it. I'm happy to help. Past few days have been great for me. I'm fed up with pottering about the house. Sick to the teeth of crosswords and word searches. It's good to be out and about, even if it's just running the odd errand or pretending to be back in the force."

That reminds Ava.

"You're a gem, Dermott. Sure, when we get Robyn settled, I can show you the picture that was left on my kitchen table?"

"Do rightly."

Hanging up shortly after and shoving her phone in her handbag, before pushing it underneath her seat, Ava hurries across the street to where she can see Robyn leaning out of the restaurant doors, waving her inside.

# Chapter Sixty-One:

After dinner's finished, Robyn continues to complain about the draught coming in every time the door opens, her jacket collar pulled up to protect her neck.

"Gone you ahead into the car, I'll get this."

"No, no. You paid for the spa and the hotel. I can at least get your dinner."

Robyn pulls out a crisp £50 note from her purse and places it on the table, before squirming deeper into her jacket as the door opens once more. Ava picks up the note and tosses her aunt her car keys.

"Gone, get yourself comfortable. I'll wait at the bar."

Silently thanking her, Robyn stands and slinks off outside. Ava joins the throng of people queuing to pay for their meal, ignoring the eyeballs from the people still waiting to get seated. It's a Saturday night, they were lucky there were only two of them or there'd be no hope of getting a table. They'd had to settle for one down by the bar, next to the kitchen and the toilets. Constantly getting elbowed by people making their way past them.

She gazes at the stairs leading up to the main seating area, thinking about the last time she was here. How she climbed them same stairs in the new shoes, believing that Mark was going to propose. The first unsettling feelings in this very place. The feelings that haven't been erased in the fortnight since. Only grew with more adding to the mix.

It takes her a while to realise that someone has stopped on the stairs and is waving at her. Cathal. He struts down the remaining stairs and joins her.

"How're you doing?" he asks after the greetings are made.

"Aye, grand. Was just in Donegal with my aunt for the night."

But I'm sure you already know that, Ava feels like saying before stopping herself. Cathal is innocent in all of this. She's too hypersensitive.

"Lovely. It nice down there?"

"Bit nippy at night, like. And the weather wasn't great. We were inside all day anyway. Getting spa treatments," Ava rests her hands under her chin and gazes to the roof dramatically.

"Oh, excuse us," Cathal snorts. "Most luxury I'd get is a bubble bath."

The two giggle before Ava asks him what he's doing here. Turning and pointing through the bannister, he shows Orla digging into an ice cream float.

"It's Orla's birthday. Big 15 today."

"Oh, that's lovely. Tell her I wish her a happy birthday. Is that who they were singing to earlier?"

Ava had saw the float with the sparklers dive past her table, but because of their position downstairs, she hadn't seen the recipient as the birthday theme had boomed over the speakers.

"One of many," Cathal rolls his eyes. "She's a bit ragin'. Must've wanted all the attention on her."

The restaurant had sung happy birthday to at least three different people, including Orla, since Ava had been seated.

"Anyway, just nipping to the bog here and then we've got to run. She's looking to have friends over tonight. Scary DVD and Christ knows what else. I'm in for a fun night."

Ava sniggers as Cathal nods to her and heads towards the toilets. Turning her attention to the bar again, she's annoyed to see someone arguing with the staff member over something on his receipt. She just wants to get home. She'd asked Dermott to be at Robyn's a good hour ago, she thinks as she checks her watch. He must be on his way over now.

She sees someone out of the corner of her eye staring at her and she freezes. Never did she think she'd feel so vulnerable in a space full of people. But when she turns in their direction, she sees it's only Mark.

"I was like *'who's that staring at me?'"* she smiles, going to grab his arm, but he swings it out of grasp. "You alright?"

Mark shakes his head, his jaw stiffened, eyes furious. She doesn't think she's ever seen him this angry before. He goes to storm off, but the restaurant's too packed and he draws to a halt, fighting to get past people. Luckily, Ava can grab his arm, but he drives on, pulling her along behind him. She apologises as she knocks into some people, their drinks spilling on the floor, as they curse after her.

When they exit the front door, he makes a right towards the town centre, but Ava gives one last hard tug and it unbalances him.

"What the fuck is wrong with you, Mark?"

"Me?" he spirals around, squaring up to her. "Me? What the fuck is wrong with *you,* Ava? You know, I actually felt sorry for you there, for a while. Using your aunt as a fuckin' sympathy card. I'm not having it any more, do you hear me? We're finished!"

Ava rushes in front of him and pushes him into the wall. Aware that people around her will think that it's a bit early on a Saturday night for this drunk couple to be having a domestic, but she doesn't care. She needs to get to the bottom of this.

"Why are you being like this? Please talk to me, Mark?"

"Oh, but I've tried, Ava. I've tried. I rang your phone and it went straight to voicemail. Sent you a text asking what you wanted to do tonight. See if we can sort something out. Hearing absolutely nothing from you, I decided I'd go out for a few drinks and dinner with the guys from work. Something I called off, may I add, for you! Texted you telling you where I'd be, but naw, that doesn't stop you. You sat down the stairs at the City Hotel with him, so why would that stop you from having a lovely meal with him here, right in front of my eyes. Eh?"

Ava's head is reeling.

"Is this about Cathal?"

"I don't give a fuck what his name is. He's bloody lucky he sulked off to the toilet, 'cause I was fit to be tied. I was ready to knock the bastard out."

Ava stares at Mark, genuinely shocked. His fists clenched. Spit on his chin from his rant. Who is this man?

"Mark... Look, I'm sorry. My phone hasn't been on all day. I've been in Donegal. I went do-"

"Oh, perfect. Going on wee romantic trips now, are yees? Well, I'm so happy for you. Don't let me stand in your way. Gone ahead. Be with him. Or is that too easy, Ava? It is, isn't it?"

"Mark, you're not listening, he's-"

"Always need a bit of drama, don't you? Just like when we started seeing each other. Your ma told you I was too old for you, so of course that made you keener. What's wrong now, eh? No drama for you? So, you decide to make some yourself. Get off with someone your own age. Act the victim when *'mysterious,'"* he air-quotes, "gifts land at your door. And you expect me to just go along with it? Believe you when you pawn them off as fuckin' threats from Boyle? Awk, sure Ava lost her ma. All load of shite going around her head. She's still grieving. Doesn't know what she wants. Abandonment issues. Do you think I came up the Foyle in a bubble? It's not on, Ave. It fuckin' isn't."

There are tears in his eyes now, his voice cracking from desperation. Losing the battle with himself.

"I'm moving forward with my life. I've a new building to get set up. I've been looking at this old house I'm interested in buying. In renovating and moving into. I thought someday you'd want to live there too. That maybe we could move forward as well. But naw, it isn't happening. Looks like it's never going to happen. I don't know what's going on in your head, Ava. If it runs in the family or whatever. But I'm not going to be here to find out. I'm sorry..."

Clearing his throat and looking around him in embarrassment, Mark turns on his heel and marches across the road to his car, perched on the pavement. Revving his engine and speeding off, Ava watches him go until the car's distorted with her tears. Settling herself onto one of the seats outside reserved for smokers, she puts her face in her hands and starts to cry hysterically.

Bradd Chambers

\*\*\*\*

When I first met Emmet, I was drunk. Another great idea, right? Again, I couldn't help it. It was Teri in work's hen-do and we were all invited. I debated going, but Ava was staying over at her friend's and the thought of going back to an empty house depressed me. I wasn't working the next day, so I thought why not?

I fairly let loose. Forgetting how much I loved the taste of drink, telling myself it'd only be for tonight. I overindulged myself with the sweet taste that always made me want more.

We had settled our troops in the Ice Wharf on the Strand Road where I had spread myself across three seats, a few drinks away from falling asleep on my chest.

"You alright there, love?"

I looked up sluggishly to see a bald man with his two front teeth chipped, his scrawny arms hanging limply from a navy checked shirt. He wasn't my type in the slightest. But then again, what right did I have to claim to have a type? And he was the first and only man who paid me any attention all night.

"Aye, and you?" I'd hiccupped.

He sat in the chair opposite and we talked a while, before he linked arms with me and thumbed down a taxi. I had no idea who had initiated it. If I'd even consented. I just went along with it.

As I slobbered into his house, I realised where this was going. But it was too late to turn back now. It didn't take long until he was on top of me. The slightest of insecurities petered out through the sweat and the alcohol. No longer shaving for beauty, but for comfort, my legs hadn't been done in a week or so, and I couldn't have imagined what shape downstairs was in. He finished pretty quickly anyway.

After an awkward few moments, I pulled my tights up and ordered another taxi. He asked for my number and I was too drunk and exhausted to give him a fake, as I typed it into his phone. A nice phone at that, one Ava was crying out to get for Christmas and Birthdays. A nice phone for quite a dank house.

I hobbled up my drive and into bed with a sickly feeling in my stomach. The last thing I remember before passing out is the screech of the message tone and the blinding glare of the phone screen as I read the message from an unknown number informing me they had fun tonight and we should do it again sometime.

Surprisingly, he got in touch not even a week later. I thought about ignoring his text, but that would've been rude. And anyway, it was the most attention I'd gotten from the opposite sex in over a decade. I quite liked it. Especially since he probably seen me in one of my worst states. It was all uphill from there.

So, I entertained the idea. We flirted over text for a few weeks. Then, one night when he was drunk, he somehow convinced me to come and collect him from town and go a drive. I pottered about the house, weighing the pros and cons of the idea, before thinking *'fuck it.'* I ran up the stairs for a quick wash and slapped on a bit of lippy.

I collected him from the Diamond, his hand on my leg before I'd even changed into second gear. Ava was in bed asleep, so I didn't chance her waking. He said we couldn't go to his, but wouldn't say why. Thoughts of a wife and kids rolling through my head. Chris's image flashing warning signals. But they slowly dispersed as his fingers travelled up my skirt.

So we did it in the car. In my passenger side seat. Where I took Ava to school the next morning. It was just as dirty and awkward as the first time. And I loved it.

After that, we coined ourselves *'fuck buddies.'* After he assured me he didn't have a wife, of course. He told me he was in between homes at that moment, and was staying with his mate. A squatter. I didn't question him. The sex was too good. And through the sex, everything else seemed to merge together too, until we were meeting up when we were both sober. And one or two times we didn't actually fuck. That's when we questioned our relationship. He told me he was falling for me, and although I didn't want to admit it, I was too.

Bradd Chambers

# Chapter Sixty-Two:

The smell of the place turns her stomach as soon as she steps foot through the door. She gets a few suspicious looks from the men slouched over the bar as she crosses the room towards them. Standing in between two vacant stools, she coughs politely at the barman, who's resting against the till, chewing gum while texting. He ignores her.

"Hi, Macka. Get the woman a drink would ye?"

One of the older guys nods down the bar towards her after a few moments of silence.

Macka looks up at her uninterestedly, before pocketing his phone and taking the two steps until he's facing her. Still chewing on the gum as if it's supplying him with nutrients.

"Erm... Hi."

He doesn't acknowledge her greeting.

"Can I have a gin and tonic, please?"

Half rolling his eyes, Macka turns and retrieves a bottle of tonic from the minifridge underneath the counter behind him, before grabbing a grubby glass and squirting in a double from the bottles attached to the wall.

"£4.80."

Ava hands him a fiver and lifts the drinks.

"Thanks. Keep the change."

"While good of ye," Macka grunts sarcastically.

Pursing her lips and ignoring the sniggers behind her, Ava decides to take the seat closest to the door and furthest from the bar. Secluded in her corner, she takes in the place. It looks like it hasn't been refurbished since the sixties. The pale wood that takes up the majority of the space is infested with damp. And although it isn't a cold night, she still feels a chill from out of nowhere in particular. The vibe, and the half a dozen Irish tri-colours, give off the notion that the ancient TV in the corner would be silenced if the English national anthem was being sang before a football match. Now she would never consider herself a snob, but this is one dive, she thinks as she lifts the glass to her lips. The smell of the glass alone is enough to make her gag.

She checks her phone before eagerly looking towards the door. He's late. She didn't know why she'd think he'd be on time. Or be waiting for her. She arrived early to give herself the upper hand. An advantage. She doesn't even know what he looks like. He could be any of the guys at the bar. He could be Macka. He could be a woman! But she doubts that anyone taking such an interest in her life would leave her at the side like this for so long. A chance she could leave. No, he's coming. Her legs jitter underneath the table and she looks down at the bubbles in her glass as she thinks back on the past few days.

The key switch had gone successfully, with Robyn being none the wiser, despite the key being a completely different colour. This is the only time Ava's been thankful for her aunt's condition. Dermott had come back with her, after wishing Robyn the best, to see the display in the kitchen. He'd pocketed the picture in a clear sandwich bag plucked from Ava's drawer. The closest thing they could get to preserving the evidence. He said he'd run it into Bratton right away.

Feeling safe with the new locks, and not wanting to arouse suspicion with Robyn, she had stayed in her own house last night. Of course, sleep didn't come easily. She lay awake for hours with her curtains open, so she could look out onto the street. She cried a little for Mark and wished she could call him, but after seeing his anger, she was too scared to even attempt contact. That wasn't the man she had fallen in love with. She knew it wasn't his fault. She had pushed him to the very edge. But it was still hard to look at him the same way. She'll try to contact him in a few days when the dust has settled.

She spent the day dipping in and out of sleep, finding comfort in the daylight. More witnesses if someone did try and get into the house. Then, shortly before dinner, she got a text from a number she didn't recognise.

*'Want answers bulls horn at 10 no cops.'*

She had tried to ring and text the number immediately, receiving no answer. She debated with herself on whether to go or not. Googling the location of the pub and seeing how long it would take her to get there. Looking for escape routes. Even searching it on Facebook to see how rough the locals were. Deciding she had nothing to lose, she left a half hour early and parked her car right opposite the pub in case she needed to make a sharp getaway.

Now here she is. In the middle of a dodgy looking pub to the west of the city. Waiting for a stranger to come and tell her why she's being victimised. Why she's being targeted. Waiting for someone who she hopes will *and* won't show up.

# Chapter Sixty-Three:

Ava waited in the Bull's Horn until shortly after midnight, before packing up and leaving, her drink untouched on the table. She's well and truly being fucked with, she thinks, as she fights with her front door. Looking down and realising she'd been trying her old key, she shakes her head as she lets herself in. The house is quiet, but that's no surprise. She didn't realise how quiet her life was until every noise made her panic. Throwing her jacket and bag down on the sofa, she switches the TV on and stares blankly at the rerun of *How I Met Your Mother*.

What had she done wrong? Why was the world punishing her? First, her dad gets up and leaves with absolutely no consideration for neither herself nor her mum, cementing her trust issues from within the womb. Growing up without a father was hard. She looked at other people's dads collecting them from school and wondered why she wasn't enough to make her dad stay. Or at least try and start or maintain a relationship with her. Then, out of the blue, her mum jumps the bridge. Leaving her parentless at the age of 17. Now, she has no idea what's going on and what she's doing wrong to receive such hatred. Scared for the future of her relationship with Mark, the business, her and Robyn's lives.

Realising that she hadn't taken her tablets this evening, after indulging herself with them over the past few days, she decides to take them with a steamy cup of hot chocolate that will hopefully also make her sleepy.

Stepping into the darkened kitchen, she turns the light on and lets out a scream. Her patio doors are covered in blood. Thick red blood covering the vast majority of the glass. Clutching her chest, she silences herself, sobbing uncontrollably.

It takes her a few moments to realise that it isn't blood. It's too watered down. Not red enough. And it's spelling something. She cranes her neck to the side, before realising that it's been written from the outside. Turning the patio lights on, she goes to reach for the door, before thinking better of it.

Fingerprints. Evidence. Tainted crime scenes. All these thoughts travel through her head as she skirts out of the front door and around the side of her house. Making sure there's no one in her back garden, she stares at the letters written on her patio doors with what she can now presume is paint. Although hard to make out due to the leaking of the paint as it travelled down the glass, mixing with other letters and points of the word, there's no denying what it spells.

*'theif!'*

*In Too Deep*

Bradd Chambers

\*\*\*\*

During the time that Emmet and I got together, I'd began to see a change in Ava. She was staying out later. Showering before and after school. Lathering herself in fragrances and body soaps. Gone were the days where she'd come back from school and throw on her pyjamas, hogging the TV. Now I was lucky to have her back for dinner, before she'd skirt off on out again. I put it down to growing up. What 17-year-old wanted to sit in with their mum?

But then I'd decided to go out the town one evening whilst I was flying solo to grab her birthday present. I'd just got paid and was saving up for a rather expensive pair of shoes in Topshop she'd been drooling over since before Christmas that I knew were on the January sales. I left the shop, rather proud of myself, knowing she'd love them. Sidestepping a gang of couples, boys in their St Columb's College uniforms hand in hand with girls in their St Cecilia's uniforms, I tottered quite close to the railings. Out of the corner of my eye, I'd thought I'd seen her. Down by The Perfume Shop. And it *was* her. Also hand in hand, but with a grown man!

My first instinct was to march straight down the escalators, grab her and drag her safely home. Out of the reach of such a perv. It took all my energy to stop myself. She would never, ever forgive me. So, I observed them. Laughing and walking along. I felt sick to my stomach. Not only because she hadn't told me, but because she'd never showed any interest in anyone before. My hopes and dreams of bringing up an asexual daughter vanished. She was growing up, and I hated it. What if he hurt her? Hurt her like Chris hurt me? What if she got pregnant? Had to bring up a kid as a single parent as I had? Especially considering she was just a kid herself. I couldn't let any of that happen.

As soon as she got home, I called her into the living room. First, I handed over her gift. It was still a week to go until her birthday, but I made up some soppy excuse that I couldn't wait to see her face any longer. Buttering her up. Daring her to lie to me. Of course, she was thrilled. But the sense of pride I knew I'd feel was soured by what came next.

"So," I'd said, perching myself on the arm of the armchair, "where've you been?"

Ava continued to admire the shoes, turning them over and over in her hand like she didn't hear me. When I refused to move the subject forward, she finally answered.

"Sorry, Mum. They're beautiful. Erm... Was just out with Amy and Molly and all at Sarah's."

The pain shot through me. Deceit from my own daughter. When did I become the mother that got lied to?

"Did you have fun in Foyleside?"

"Aye, we just lay about and watched T..." Ava's head jolted up from the shoes, her eyes widened.

"I saw you... And that boy. *Man,* should I say?"

I'm not proud of what came next. One of the worst fights we ever had. The screams could definitely be heard by the neighbours, but we had to have it out. I couldn't let her get hurt. Get her heart broken. Eventually, it fizzled out. I couldn't believe I'd actually banned her from seeing him, forcing her to scale the stairs in tears, banging the bedroom door behind her.

Bradd Chambers

# Chapter Sixty-Four:

Settling down at her desk, Ava loads her computer and is set on being present for a good day at work today. She's been too distracted lately. She can't lose this business. Or the volunteers. They're what help her drive this charity. She can't seem like she's slacking off. They'll all turn on her. Like everyone else has. That's why, today, she's arrived in an hour early. Making a statement that she's the first to arrive. A new week, a new Ava, she thinks, knowing it sounds ridiculous, especially given her current circumstances.

She has the photos of last night's graffiti resting in her phone. She refused to ring Dermott, not at that time of the night. He'd done too much for her already. She'll ring him today at lunch time and ask him to come in for a chat. She'll show him everything then. She sat on her sofa all night last night with the TV on mute just in case whoever it was came back. She had half an urge to go out there and start scrubbing it off. Scared of what the neighbours behind her would think or say. But she needed to leave it untouched. She even stood a good bit of distance away from it to take the photos.

She waited all night until it was appropriately acceptable to get ready and drive into work without anyone asking questions. Whoever texted her, looking to meet in the pub, clearly wanted her out of the house. That can be presumed from the inability to spell *'thief'* correctly, she thinks, as the spelling and grammar of both the e-mail and text weren't great. Were they looking to get into the house again? Was this her comeuppance for changing the locks? Or was this their plan all along?

Questions she will discuss with Dermott in a few hours, she thinks. But until then, she has some work to do. They have enough money now to rent a space in the city. Get it set up for counselling sessions and the likes. Searching for properties on one tab, the other open on their official Facebook page. She looks at the number of likes and followers they have. Someone's bound to know something. She thinks about writing a status, asking for whoever the (not so) charitable person is to come forward. That way, she can find out if this is what's wrong. If she's being punished for *'stealing.'* But she decides against it. If this all came out, it would ruin the business. She would never be taken seriously again. She needs this charity to thrive. For people to relate to it. To save people's lives.

The volunteers dwindle in one by one. Discussions of weekends over cups of tea makes the office seem almost normal, Ava thinks. Her home life absolutely nowhere near the sort. It takes a half hour of everyone being present, typing away furiously on their keyboards, when Michael recognises it.

"Jesus, Ave. What's happened your desk?"

Ava skids her chair out to get a closer look. The third drawer down has been battered and loosely sandwiched back in. The one Ava locks to keep important and confidential documents inside. How had she not noticed this before? She blames the lack of sleep, as she fingers the damage, causing the whole drawer to collapse onto the floor. And shoved carelessly back inside, lying open and empty, is the money tin that they had used at the charity night last week.

# Chapter Sixty-Five:

"Long time no see."

Ava twists around to see the locksmith from the other day pottering into her office, his toolkit clanging clumsily off one of the desks.

"Aw, Jesus... I'm so sorry, I've completely forgotten your name."

"Alan," he plonks down his tools and stretches a dirty hand out as if this is the first time they've met.

She takes it delicately.

"So, what's the craic here, then?"

He steps through into the back hallway, even tinier now that so many people have been clambering in and out of it. Michael, Paddy and Claire still examining the damage.

"Got broken into last night," Ava nods towards the back door, despite her being behind him, and the fact that he can obviously see that for himself.

Was it a rhetorical question?

"Came in this morning to this," Michael shakes his head.

"Scumbags. Anything taken?"

"Luckily not," she says, squeezing herself through the horde of people to the kitchen and boiling the kettle for the fifth time this morning. "Although my desk has been broken into as well. All our donation money had been resting in there, but thankfully Michael took it around the corner to the bank before closing time on Friday."

He whistles.

"Very lucky. You made twelve grand the other night if you believe everything you read in the papers. Aye?"

"We did, aye."

She cleans and refills a mug previously gratefully received by a police officer. She hadn't wanted to contact the police, rather do it discreetly through Dermott. But, of course, she had to show the other volunteers that she was doing something about it. If this had happened anyone else in any different situation, of course the police would've been called. Alan gets to work with repairing the door as she hands him over his tea.

"Ta," he takes a sip. "Funny though."

"Excuse me?"

"I'm saying it's funny. Five computers in here and none of them were taken. And your desk being the only one targeted. Now I'm no expert, but it almost seems like whoever broke in knew exactly what they were looking for... And where."

"Hmmm," Ava fidgets, her own mug pressed to her lips. "Strange."

"Well anyway, no point stressing on the past. Did ya get a chance to speak to your uncle?"

From one awkward conversation to another, Ava thinks.

"Naw, I'm afraid. Just left my aunt's shortly after you did."

None of it is a lie, she tells herself.

"I meant to send him a wee text there the other day. Haven't saw him in yonks. We always used to go for a pint after a job together. Lovely man, your uncle."

Ava nods before she realises his back is to her.

"Aye, he is surely."

She watches him working for a few minutes longer before her phone goes. She expects it to be Cathal. Word had spread fast that the local charity had been burgled, and he had already texted her to ask if they were okay. A story at the core of the concern, she's sure. But half because of what happened with Mark the other night and half because of not having time with the chaos of it all, she had failed to text him back. Oddly enough, it isn't him. It's Robyn.

"Alright, Rob. In the middle of something her-"

"Ava, please. I need you at the house right away. Please, come help me. It's important!"

# Chapter Sixty-Six:

"Come on, come on, come on!" Ava screams at the traffic lights at the crossroads on Columba Terrace.

After Robyn hung up on her, she sprinted from the office, shouting to the others that she had another aunt related emergency. She doesn't care if they don't believe her. All that matters now is Robyn.

The lights turn green and she floors the accelerator, spinning her wheels as she heads straight for Limavady Road. A million thoughts and situations going through her head. Is she okay? Is she just confused? It's been a while since one of her episodes, maybe it has come back with a vengeance? It wouldn't be the first time she rang her like that.

But, no. It is. She has never been so forceful. So frightened. Has something horrible happened? Has whoever targeted Ava's house last night targeted hers too? Is he there now? Hurting her? She doubts she would be able to phone. Maybe he made her phone? His way of luring her there? Intent on stealing back the money? She doesn't know. All she knows is she has to get there as fast as she can.

She makes the short journey in record time, jumping out of her car, leaving the engine running and the keys in the ignition. Sprinting up Robyn's drive, she curses herself for her stupidity in forgetting her keys, before making a decision that the back would be faster. Dodging the front door entirely, she skirts around the house and flies through the back door, which is, thankfully, unlocked. She comes to a rest in the living room, in front of Robyn who is in her normal armchair by the fireplace.

"What's – wrong?" she gasps for breath, clasping her oncoming stitch.

Robyn stares at her with a blank expression on her face, the initial startle of her bursting through diminished. Ava stares at her a while longer before groaning, exasperated. Nothing's wrong. She's just in one of her moods.

"Robyn, for fuck sake. Are you serious? You scared the shit out of me. I nearly killed myself on the way over here. You seriously trying t-"

A cough from the kitchen silences her. Her ears perk up, joining the hairs on the back of her neck as she senses someone behind her. She had barrelled through so carelessly that she hadn't had time to check her surroundings. All her attention on finding her aunt. She turns around precariously and gasps. Because there, stood right in front of her, although looking dramatically different with her short, spiky black hair and thick rimmed glasses that obscure the majority of her face, is her mother.

*In Too Deep*

Bradd Chambers

\*\*\*\*

Emmet and I were in a relationship for six months before I agreed that he could meet Ava. He was the first man I was bringing into her life, I didn't want to make any mistakes. Kept telling me he was great with kids and convinced me she'd fall in love with him too.

So, I invited him around for dinner one Friday night. But Ava never showed up at four from off the bus. I left it until after five before I gave her a call, but it went straight to voicemail. I worried frantically. This wasn't like Ava. Emmet landed at dinner time and I stirred the big pot of stew, knowing it was past boiling point, definitely sticking to the arse of the pot. But she never showed.

She finally rang me back shortly before nine. Me jumping off the sofa as if Emmet's arm around me was barbed wire.

"Sorry, Mum. My phone was out of battery, only getting a charger now I'm at Ciara's."

"Where have you been? I've been out of my mind. You had me so worried, Ave."

Her teenage groan came through the phone.

"I told you. I was at Ciara's. I had no way to contact you. I'm sorry!"

The last word was half-shouted, as if she were daring me to confront her. Question her.

"I'd made stew."

Silence.

"And what?"

"Thought it would be nice for us all to sit down together as a family."

I could feel the tension over the phone.

"'*All?'* Mum, what's the big deal? I've stayed at other people's houses for dinner before? What's so special about tonight?"

I stared at Emmet resting his feet on the coffee table, his eyes on the TV.

"I... I just thought it'd be nice. When are you home?"

There was shuffling as the phone was moved about.

"Ciara's mum said she'll leave me home later on."

"But you said you *were* at Ciara's, so where are you now?"

Another few seconds of silence.

"Er... We're out in the car. Going to the shops."

There was no background noise. It was perfectly quiet. If it weren't for her delays in answers I may not have noticed. The silence was deafening. Not so much as a hum of an engine or a radio turned down low.

"Don't lie to me, Ava. Where are you?"

"I told you," she insisted, after another few seconds of mumbling.

"You're with that boy, aren't you?"

"No!"

"Don't lie to me, Ava. You know what I've said about him. He's too old."

"I'm 17, Mum. I can do whatever the fuck I want!"

She hung up the phone, leaving me flustered as I tried to think of a comeback. I'd turned around and Emmet was on his feet.

"Think it's best if I'm not here when she comes back. Wouldn't be the best introduction," he chuckled.

I'd nodded.

"I think this is a sign. She's not ready."

He looked at me confused.

"She didn't know anything abo-"

"I know. But it just shows that things aren't great. We can't add something else into the mix. Not now. I'm not ready, I should've said. I don't think I was tonight, either."

Emmet looked annoyed but hid it well. Nodding and squeezing my arm, he kissed my forehead before leaving me alone in the living room. The front door snapped shut behind him, making me flinch.

Bradd Chambers

# Chapter Sixty-Seven:

Ava stares at her in disbelief. Different hair. Unnecessary glasses. More, deeper lines across her face. But the same loving eyes. The same tiny mouth. The same arms opening out for her to run into. But she doesn't. She *was* the woman from the charity night in St Columb's Park. She knew she looked familiar. She was right. Second guessed herself, putting it down to stress and her lack of sleep. She should've gone with her instinct.

Once the initial shock departs, her rage flares. Ava marches over and slaps her across the face. Robyn struggles out of her chair and attempts to restrain Ava as she pelts her fists down on her mum, cowering beneath her.

"What the fuck?" Ava shouts, Robyn trying to *'sssh'* her, but she keeps kicking and screaming, desperate to get out of her clutch.

Get at the woman who claimed to be her mum. The woman who left her depressed and miserable for years. The woman she thought was swallowed up by the river. Like so many are. The anger of her suicide converting and intensifying by the realisation that she didn't kill herself at all. Who would do something like this? Put their family, and especially their only daughter, through this?

She had dreamed of this day. Wished for this day. Wanting to see her, to speak to her, one more time. But in all those scenarios, she never once felt the way she does now. They embraced, kissed and caught up. Never letting go of one another. Always wanting to somehow touch the other to confirm that it was real. But the thought of her own mother even standing in the same room as her right now is turning Ava's stomach.

"Ava, please," her mum's eyes are filling with tears as Robyn finally manages to pull her away.

As are Ava's.

"Ave, you need to calm down. Please, for me, calm down," Robyn has her mouth pressed against her ear.

"Rob, she did this. She knew all along-"

"I know, I know."

"-what she done. She pretended to kill herself, Rob. What sick-"

"I know, Ave. I know."

"-bitch does something like that? It's unforgivable. Unexplainable. It's..."

Slowly, Ava stops squirming, turning her attention on her aunt. When it seems like she's calmed down, Robyn groans, relaxing her muscles and stepping away from Ava. Ava slides to the ground, jolting her stare between Robyn and Fiona. Her aunt and her mother.

"You..." she swallows. "You know?... You knew!"

The sisters share a look before returning their attention to the floor. To Ava.

"Aye, darling. But it's complicated. It's-"

"No..." Ava darts up onto the chair on the other side of the room and away from their oncoming gestures. "No. You said you saw her jump off. You waited in the ambulance. You got her texts. You saw... You saw..."

Then it all comes flooding back. Her anger rising once more. Directed towards her aunt this time.

"You saw me cry myself to sleep. You saw how it affected me. How hurt I was. How absolutely fucking heartbroken I was. How hopeless I felt. You took me to the doctors to get antidepressants and anxiety tablets and fuck knows what else. You left me to my counsellor appointments. Picked me up again. And... And the whole time... You fucking knew!" she spits the last word.

Now Robyn is crying. All three girls can't take their leaking eyes off each other. They just cry and stare. Each one wanting to speak, but not wanting to be the first to break the silence.

# Chapter Sixty-Eight:

Fiona sits facing her daughter at Robyn's kitchen table. Her sister resting between them like a referee. Ready to jump into action in case Ava becomes violent again. Three cups of untouched tea sit in front of them, the steam coming off them evaporating in the silence.

"Ava, I cannot apologise enough. I really can't."

Ava glares at her, her chin protruded forward. Looking the spit of her father.

"I don't even know if I want to know what happened..." Ava struggles the words out, her voice finally broken from the angry shouts and sobs.

"You deserve to know. Please, Ava. I won't let you leave without at least knowing *why* I did it."

Ava continues to give her daggers, before mustering a subtle nod.

"That night I... Died-"

Ava's eye twitches.

"- Do you remember me ringing you? Asking why you didn't come home?"

Ava's eyes glaze over with tears again. Of course she remembers, it replays over and over in her head.

"I didn't tell you this because I was scared. Scared for you and scared for myself. After what happened with your father... I decided I deserved to be happy. And I was... I met a man. Emmet, he was called."

Ava's ears perk up, her attention grasped by the name of the man from the e-mail.

"I was seeing him for a few months before he, somehow, convinced me to introduce him to you. Bring him into our little unit. He came over that night and you didn't come home. When I rang, you were with that older man. The one I wasn't happy about you seeing. I understand now, you've ended up with him?"

Ava blinks. What way does she answer that? Thankfully, her mother doesn't press her.

"Don't worry. You don't have to lie anymore. I've seen you together. You have my full blessing. You look so happy. I'm so sorry for judging him. I'm genuinely glad you found someone decent. Something I never could do."

Ava manages a half smile, her heart yearning for Mark.

"Emmet left about a half hour before you came home. Before we... Fell out."

The shouts and roars toss between them as they remember the events of their final night together. Robyn only being able to imagine what they're seeing.

"When you went up to bed, I got a text from Emmet telling me to come out a drive with him. I was so angry with you, I just left. That's when he told me everything..."

Fiona breathes out dramatically, biting her clenched fist.

"He was being hunted down. By a gang in the city. Mistaken identity, he told me. It seemed that his friends had gotten into a spot of bother with some dodgy business. Stealing pirate DVDs, money and other stuff from a local shop. He didn't go into too much detail, I wasn't sure he even knew himself.

"Well, turns out that they'd stolen from the wrong man. The gang... They'd kneecapped one boy, trying to get him to talk. The boy gave over Emmet's name. To protect his real bosses. A mole, if you will, who knew Emmet in the group contacted him. Telling him to run. They'd said they'd kill him. Emmet apparently did a bit of business with them a few years before. Nothing illegal, he'd told me... But it seemed they'd regarded him as an ally. And him betraying them was something that they didn't take well. He told him to *'take his missus'* too because they were talking about targeting her... Me!"

Ava's confused expression is prominent on her face. Robyn just stares forward, the information seemingly old news to her.

"So you chose him over me?"

"No! Ava, honestly. Please, keep listening to me," she begs as Ava deliberates leaving. "He told me we had to go. I told him he was mad. That I wasn't leaving, but he said I was stupid not to. Said I didn't know who I was dealing with. Some right dodgy bastards, apparently. They had contacts, and they were probably already scoping out my information as we spoke. That I wouldn't be safe.

That you wouldn't be safe. I had to go on the run with him.

"You have to believe me, Ava. I tried to think of every solution. He laughed at me when I suggested the police. He said there's no way they would give him a second to defend or explain himself if he tried to contact the gang to plead his innocence. And without the name of who was really behind it, that was useless anyway, even if they did listen. His friends had already gone into hiding in fear of being attacked for his whereabouts, or thinking they were involved too.

"I had no idea what to do. Whether to go in and grab you. Bring you with me. But he told me that we were too involved in the community. Had people that would miss us. Ask questions. He came from a part around town where people disappeared and reappeared like clockwork. It was just the norm. No-one was ever even asked where they'd gone. He wouldn't be missed. I was a different matter, though. I had to come with him to protect myself, and to protect you. But I couldn't just disappear. That would leave you to be pursued.

"No, I had to properly disappear off the face of the earth. Leave no rock unturned or any questions unanswered. I knew what he meant before he said it. I just knew... I knew that I'd have to fake my suicide."

# Chapter Sixty-Nine:

Ava's stare jolts between both of her mother's eyes, circulating her face. Searching for any signs of dishonesty. Unloyalty. Although she's spent the past three years away from her, she never forgot her face. Her mannerisms. After all, at one point she was all she had. Leaning back in her chair, Ava crosses her arms.

"I think I believe you..."

Fiona lets out a sigh of relief, beginning to stand.

"... It doesn't mean that I am one bit happy with you," comes Ava's curt ending.

Fiona nods hysterically, returning her bum to the seat and her elbows to the table.

"Of course, darling. Of course."

"So," Ava turns her attention to her aunt. "Where did you come into this?"

Robyn's eyes remain on the tablecloth, slowly fingering a rip in the material.

"Your mum came straight here after meeting Emmet and told me everything. Begged me to promise not to tell anyone. To keep it a secret. Of course, I took the information like you just did. Only, I could have stopped her. But..." she

glances over at her sister, who nods knowingly. "...
She was relentless. Said she wouldn't have any
harm come to you. If they were seeking her out,
they would find you. We came up with the plan...
She sent me the texts and I waited at the
roundabout before the new bridge for her signal."

Robyn's eyes start to well up again.

"Believe me, Ave. There were so many times
I wanted to tell you... But I just couldn't break that
promise. I had to keep you safe."

"Is that why you're... The way you are?" Ava
fights back her anger.

Robyn nods sullenly.

"I *knew* it seemed like you were putting it
on sometimes."

Robyn's mouth falls open slightly.

"Only sometimes, pet. The times when I had
to get my way out of an awkward conversation or
situation. But I swear, the drink and the drugs have
played havoc with me. I'm sorry I put you through
that, I really am. But it just seemed to be the only
way I could cope... With everything."

She sniffs, lifting a tissue to blow her nose.

"So, why now?" Ava narrows her eyes at her
mother. "Why come back?"

Fiona reaches her hands across the table,
but Ava ignores them.

"Well... That night I... Left... Emmet told me
he had a friend with a house in Belfast. That we
could stay there for a while to get back on our feet.
So, we pulled up at the garage at the bottom of the
Glenshane and used the toilets."

She physically grimaces at the memory. Thinking back on hiding under the blanket in the back of his car.

"He made me cut my hair and put on these glasses and clothes that make me look about ten years older than what I am," she chuckles, before realising no-one else is amused. "We squatted in his mates in South Belfast for a while, before he managed to get us a house in the east. He got a job almost immediately, but told me it was too risky for me to get one. After all, I had no ID, no national insurance... Nothing. I had to stay at home. Obviously, I went stir crazy. Had such bad cabin fever.

"So, I started to leave the house. Nothing mad, like. Just a trip to the shops and that. Grab a pint of milk from the Tescos around the corner. I wasn't even allowed there, Emmet made me order in an ASDA delivery at the start of every week. I was proper secluded for so long. If we ever went anywhere, I had to stay in the car. I told him time and time again that I had no contacts in any part of Belfast, but he wouldn't listen.

"Needless to say, our relationship became strained. Around this time last year, I decided enough was enough. Throwing on sunglasses, I started to go into the town centre. I had no money, of course, I just wanted to potter about. It was so nice, seeing people. Being treated like a real human. Being in the big open world.

"Then... About two months ago, I ran into someone in Victoria Square. No-one I knew, but he seemed to know me. Asked if I was living with

Emmet, and I panicked. Told him I didn't know who he was talking about and tried to skirt off, but he persisted. Told me Emmet was a very bad man and I should get away from him. After a while, I started to humour him. Just to see if we were talking about the same Emmet. He told me that Emmet didn't have a job, despite leaving the house all day and coming back at tea time. He told me he was a drug dealer. And he'd supplied his son with so many drugs that he'd overdosed and died a few months before."

Robyn gasps lightly, shaking her head.

"I told him he had the wrong guy. But he promised me. Said he followed his son's friends that Saturday night after the funeral and he saw Emmet supplying near City Hall. He followed Emmet to our house and saw me through the window. I wondered why he didn't go to the police, but he told me that that's not how people around his parts dealt with things. I promised him that I had no idea... I mean, he used to come and go as he pleased. I had no authority over him, but he wasn't out of the house so much at night that I would ever be suspicious of something like that.

"As soon as Emmet left for whatever he disappeared to do the next day, I searched the house. I didn't know what I was looking for. Drugs... Money... Whatever. I remembered the nights he said he was going out. And I lay half-awake as he woke me barrelling in through the front door. He'd always go into the downstairs spare bedroom. So, I turned the place upside down looking, but couldn't find anything. Giving up, I sat on the bed and

thought about what sort of person I'd become...
Whenever I just... I just knew. Looking at the chest
of drawers, I slid it out from against the wall and,
sure enough, there was a tiny square door etched
into the wall that was almost entirely missable if
you weren't looking. It was so overly painted over
you could barely make out the tiny dent, only big
enough for a finger nail to fit into, and I was able to
swing it open discreetly. There, I found thousands
and thousands of pounds stashed inside the tiny
cupboard. Huge wads of notes.

"I slammed the door shut straight away, and
resumed the room to its original position, before
running out into the back garden. I had no idea
what I was going to do. I couldn't ring the police, I
was supposed to be dead! And I couldn't confront
him because he'd began to become so violent
towards me. I was scared..."

She fans her eyes and gazes at the picture
frames on the cupboard, reflecting easier times.

"In the end, I decided I would play him at his
own game. It's amazing how ignorant our lives are.
Like when I was washing the dishes, I heard him go
into that downstairs bedroom and lock the door
behind him. It happened several times throughout
the weeks, and that was the only times I noticed.
God knows how many more times there were. How
oblivious I was. So, every morning, when he'd get
up and leave... I'd sneak in and steal a few notes
out of different wads. Make him think he'd
miscounted or was paid wrongly.

"That added up until I went into town and
bought myself a phone. Just a standard

smartphone so I could look up the internet unobserved by him. Wouldn't dare try on the laptop in case he checked the search history. That's when I started searching for you, and my heart broke when I realised how you'd grown up. You're so beautiful. And then I saw all the articles about making the charity, and in my name. I mean, I was honoured, despite the guilt. And I just really wanted to see you. I tried phoning Robyn a few times, but she was never in," she grabs hold of her sister's hand. "Just to check up on everyone, you know? I never could before. My phone and everything ended up in the Foyle."

Ava struggles to fight back more tears collecting in her eyes. Her mother had gone through so much. And yet she couldn't extinguish the fire in her heart that flamed her rage.

"I started to come up with a plan," Fiona continues. "To track his movements and count the money, see if there was a certain day he'd get a load or days he took it to his big bosses. Some form of a routine. Get the money and runaway, come here and get you. Maybe move away until he was caught... Wishful thinking, I know. But with so much time on my hands, I daydreamed so much, you have no idea.

"And then... A few weeks ago... I was woken in the middle of the night by a crash downstairs. Emmet was gone. After finally convincing myself that no one was in the house, I made it downstairs to see the living room window was smashed, and lying on the sofa was a brick with a message tied to it saying: *'murdering scum.'* I just couldn't believe it. Had he killed someone else through supplying? Or what else was he not telling me? So, I packed up all I could, before scoffing a large amount of the drug money and left. Called a taxi from around the corner that took me to the bus station, although I had to wait another few hours for the bus.

"And since then, I've been renting an Airbnb out near Lettershandoney. Just to keep myself away from the crowd, but I couldn't help but come in now and then. Like to your house," she clasps her fingers together and rests them on her chin, staring at her daughter admirably. "I'm so sorry if I seem creepy or stalkerish."

Despite herself, Ava finds herself smiling shyly.

"So... The Letter with the lily?"

Fiona nods her head, beaming.

"The new shoes?"

"Bought them for myself with that bastard's money. You made me so proud that I thought you deserved them more. You looked so gorgeous in them."

"So... You were following me?"

Fiona blows out.

"I wouldn't say full time, no. But I would watch from afar sometimes, just to see you. To feel close to you."

"And the charity event?"

Fiona blinks.

"I saw you there... With a pile of girls."

Her mother reddens.

"I tried to keep my distance. To fit in with the crowd. Clearly it didn't work," she laughs.

Ava surprises herself by joining in, letting herself be absorbed in the madness.

Bradd Chambers

\*\*\*\*

We continue to sit at Robyn's kitchen table for a while longer, talking about the woes of the world that tore us apart. Catching up with everything that's been going on. It's amazing to be this close to Ava. Within touching distance. After observing her for weeks. Thinking about her every day for three years. After the awkward silences become unbearable, all avenues of conversation perused, Ava takes a quick glance at her phone and mumbles something about having to return to work.

"Shit," she spits, rushing out of the front door.

I watch from the window as she climbs into the front seat and kills the ignition, clambering out and over the trimmed grass.

"Has that been on the whole time?" I laugh.

My Ava. Always so clumsy. Something she got from me.

"Aye, I was in such a rush to get in. I thought..." Ava shudders.

"You thought what, darling?"

"So, that five grand we mysteriously received on the charity night," Ava ignores me, cocking her head to the side, closing the door behind her for a slither of privacy. "That was you?"

I look bashfully to my feet.

"It was. I gave it to a little boy who scooted past me. Told him to tell your colleague it was from his daddy. It isn't near enough after what I put you through, but it's a start. I didn't want to spend it all because I didn't know how long I'd be here before I found the courage to see you. To come to Robyn's. I had to make sure Damien wasn't here."

Ava flinches and glances towards the living room, where Robyn has resumed her usual position in her chair. She looks like she wants to tell me something, but decides against it. Maybe too much has been shared today already?

"And Mr Ted?"

I frown.

"Mr Ted... That old thing you used to carry about when you were younger? What about him?"

"You didn't take him from here," she frowns, pointing to the roof, "and leave him at the backdoor of my office?"

I stare at her perplexed.

"No. Why would I do such a thing?"

Ava's eyes expand.

"It must've been Emmet," she bites her lip.

My heart stops.

"Emmet? What?!"

She gazes at me, the crease on her forehead from frowning the only thing tainting her beautiful features.

"Yeah... Emmet's... Erm... Been in touch..."

I instantly feel like a huge object has fallen onto me. I crash down onto the stairs, unable to withhold my own weight as Ava screams.

Robyn hobbles out, reaching for me but I *'shoo'* her away. Resting my head in my hands, I think through the situation. What has he done? What is he going to do?

When I find my energy moments later, I slide my hands down my face and look up at Ava. My gorgeous daughter.

"What has he done? I left subtly. I've left no trace that I've been here."

Robyn and Ava share concerned glances.

"What's happened, love?" Robyn stares at Ava.

Ava blows out, fidgeting with her hands before sighing and closing the door properly.

# Chapter Seventy:

"This is all my fault. This is all my fault."

Fiona does laps of Robyn's tiny kitchen as Ava's story comes to a close, finishing on rushing over because she thought her aunt was in danger. Robyn gazes at her with hurt in her eyes.

"I can't believe all of that was going on and you never thought to tell me."

"I'm sorry, Rob. I didn't want to scare you or upset your moods. I was looking out for you, trying to protect you," she echoes the emotional responsibility that her aunt had harboured for her over these past few years.

"So," her mother comes to a stop in the living room, "here's what I think has happened. When he found me missing, and obviously a lot of his cash gone, he came looking for me. Derry would've been the first place to look. Somewhere I know well, I've barely been out of the city to go anywhere else. He's obviously been keeping an eye on both of your houses. And-"

"But how did he get in here?" Ava interrupts with a whine, tapping her feet off the rug in frustration.

"The spare key?" Robyn offers.

Fiona steals a glance at Robyn, before covering her mouth.

"I'm so sorry, Rob."

Robyn looks so confused that if she hadn't made her brash confession only an hour before, Ava would believe she was going through one of her moments.

"Sorry for what?"

"It was... It..."

Letting out a sharp cry, Fiona flops herself down on the settee beside Ava, who coils unintentionally away from her. Instinct taking over.

"When Emmet and I started to see each other... We came here a few times. Just to get away from it all. For a proper bed..."

She chews the inside of her mouth and grips the sofa cushions tightly. Giving Ava the impression that it wasn't just the bed. Her stomach starts to turn as she realises they did it right here, before remembering that they would've did it on the bed she stayed in upstairs too. Bile collecting in her throat.

"How did you know about the spare key?" Robyn looks shocked.

"You mentioned it in passing years ago. I never thought anything of it. I didn't even remember about it until one time when we were driving around looking for a spot, and I saw your house from the bridge. I'm so sorry, he obviously saw me pick the key from underneath the gnome."

"That's how he got in," Ava shakes her head.

It's all starting to make sense. And through getting into this house, he was able to snaggle her keys as well.

"So... Why give back my keys and not Robyn's spare?"

The trio think for a second.

"Think about it," Fiona snaps her fingers. "You'd miss yours. But no one would miss Robyn's."

"But why not make a spare? Like he must've done with mine?"

Fiona's mouth twitches as she shrugs, putting her head in her hands once again.

"I'm sorry," she manages to muffle.

"It's okay, I've changed the locks." Ava goes to pat her mother on the back, but changes her mind halfway through. "He can't get into either house. That's probably why he left that message on my patio doors."

Fiona jerks up again.

"Aye! That's it. So," she jumps up onto her feet and starts doing her circuits around the kitchen once more, this time including the table. "He comes looking for me, obviously targeting you two. Then, steals Mr Ted as a threat to hand me over, if you will."

"But how would he know about Mr Ted?"

"Oh, we talked about everything. I must've brought it up at some point. Anyway, that was the night after the charity night, right?"

Ava nods.

"Then, when here is empty for the night when Robyn's in hospital, he sneaks in and obviously steals your keys to make a copy. If they were in your bag, he caught sight of the picture and doctored it as another threat. We don't know how long that photo could've been sitting on your table. Then he tries to ring you at work, maybe to intimidate you into telling him where I was. That's why he refused to speak to your colleagues.

"The next day, he sends that e-mail because he reads about the large donation in the Letter, possibly knowing that it was from me, and that's why he talks about hurting me in it. You go on the run with Robyn, get the locks changed and he can't find you. I mean, I came looking a few times at both houses and couldn't see anything. I'm so lucky I didn't bang into him," she waves away her selfishness. "Sorry. Then he texts you to meet him last night, maybe to break into your house again? When he can't get in, he writes on your patio doors as another threat. As well as breaking into your office to try and steal back the money, and then some..."

Even as the picture starts to build, it sends Ava's mind into overdrive. How has she become involved in this? This is something you see in action or mystery films, not in the tiny city of Derry.

"Why don't we get in touch with the lads that are looking for him? Maybe they can take him off our hands?"

Ava can't believe the words that are coming out of her mouth. She sounds like a gangster. Fiona shakes her head anyway.

"I couldn't tell you who they are. He never said. Clearly, in retrospect, I've realised that it mustn't be false identity, that he *had* been dabbling in similar things here, and got involved with the wrong crowd. Or pissed off the wrong people."

"Then what should we do, Mum?" Ava pleas.

It's the first time she's called her mum all afternoon, making her feel like a teenager again. The loose connection starts to stutter back to life as the two stare into one another's eyes.

"I don't know, pet. But I'll sort it. Don't worry. In the meantime, you best get back to work. It's nearly time you closed up. We can't have anyone asking questions, and I think this goes without saying, but please don't tell anyone about me."

Ava turns to Robyn.

"What about Dermott? He could help?"

Robyn shakes her head.

"We can't risk it, pet."

Ava nods, picking herself up off the sofa and coming face to face with Fiona as she blocks the exit, her arms outstretched. Awkwardly, Ava allows herself to be enveloped in them. Suddenly, the tension in her body evaporates as the familiar feelings creep back, running through her arteries, circulating them around her body from her heart. She's shocked to find her own arms wrapping around her mother.

After several moments, she pulls away as she feels tears prick at her eyes once more.

"Are you safe here?" she coughs.

Fiona and Robyn share a split-second glance of worry before nodding and doing a terrible job of reassuring her they'll be fine.

"Just look out for his car," Fiona walks her to the door. "It's a black BMW. 520S or something like that,"

Emmet's choice of e-mail now makes sense, Ava thinks. And that must've been the car outside her house the other day. She crosses the threshold, her mother hidden in the shadows of the door

"Take care of yourself, love. And stay in touch through Robyn. Or Twitter."

Ava turns around confused, before a lightbulb moment.

*"'heathermoore71?'"*

Her mother beams.

"Yeah. My middle name, Grandma's maiden name and the year I was born. Was it not obvious?" she chuckles.

"Not even a little bit," Ava smiles before waving at the closing door and crossing the grass once more to her car.

Strapping herself in, it takes her a few minutes to start the car as she thinks back on the events of the past few hours. She's being hunted down by a violent criminal. Her life and those of her loved ones are in danger. But, most importantly, her mum is back. She's alive. However, it came at a cost.

# Chapter Seventy-One:

Despite knowing that the coast is clear, Ava still creeps into every room. Leaving no wardrobe door unopened. No under bed unchecked. Unlocking and relocking the doors several times like some form of OCD. Everything is just how she left it this morning. When she's convinced she's alone and safe, only then does she run the bath. The warm soapy water feels good on her tired skin as she soaks into the tub. What. A. Day.

    The guys at the office didn't even ask how Robyn was or what had happened. Either getting used to it now or just beyond caring, Ava didn't mind. Hopefully soon it will all be out in the open and she won't have to sneak around anymore. She'd found it hard to concentrate when she sat back down at her desk for the last 20 minutes of the day. Still staring at the same letting agency website. Turning things over in her head. She barely heard the volunteers call out their goodbyes and didn't realise she was last in the office. Deciding she'd not get any work done even if she stayed there all night, she thought a bath and some alone time with her thoughts was just what she needed.

She tries to ignore the negative probing at the side of her head, wondering what she's going to do about Emmet. He could be walking behind her in the street and she wouldn't have the first clue. She has no idea what he looks like. She tries to focus on the fact that her mother is alive and well... But when you're getting targeted by a lunatic with a history of violence, it's hard to do. She decided against contacting Dermott about the vandalism, whilst she washed the graffiti off her patio doors. He'd ask too many questions. And she never had the best poker face. Couldn't lie to save her life.

Her mum personal messaged her on Twitter under her pseudonym telling her to take care and she loved her. She felt weird leaving her on read, but she needs to ease back into it. Finding it hard to forget that they're not talking from beyond the grave. It has been a long three years, and a lot to take in over the space of a few hours.

The ping of her phone bounces off the tiles and around the bathroom. Squelching an arm out of the bath, she dries it indolently on a towel before reaching for her phone. Intent on just glancing at the message and returning to her bath, she gasps as she jolts upright, her body squeaking off the tub.

*'bulls horn now no cops if u want ur ma and ant alive.'*

*In Too Deep*

Bradd Chambers

****

We're sitting on the sofa watching *Coronation Street* when it happens. The shadow passes the blinds, making me jump. Robyn's head shoots in my direction as she mutes the TV. I dive for the light, although it's too late. We huddle behind the sofa, the only place clear of view from the back-door window. The only way to see in. We clutch each other's hands concerningly as we imagine him trudging across the stones and opening the gate. Feet falling on gravel as he makes his way to the back door. Key in hand.

     Almost as if on cue, we hear the subtle sound of a key entering a lock. Moaning slightly, Robyn covers her mouth with her jumper, like that will stifle her sounds, before nestling further into me. The new lock blocks the key's interactions. The old handle shakes. I can almost picture it. Refusing to give way. Protecting us. Still it rattles on. We hear the effort being put into it, and the bangs as his body weight is slammed against the door.

     This goes on for several moments, before, startling us, Robyn's house phone goes. Piercing the air. That same old school ring. The kind people put as their ringtone on their mobiles for a laugh.

The rings penetrate the living room, the next one coming before the echo from the original stops.

Like the door, he won't budge. He won't take no for an answer. I've learned that about him. Once he wants something, he gets it. But he isn't getting into this house. He's not getting my family. Or me. Does he know I'm here? Teasing and toying with me? Or does he still have no clue?

The phone finally stops just to blare out a split second later. Someone really wants to get in touch with Robyn. Maybe it's Damien? Or maybe it's Ava? I pray she's okay, as I clutch Robyn close to me. They're all I have left. How could I have ever left them? Especially for the monster still trying to break down the kitchen door? I'll make it up to them. I have to. He won't get the better of me.

*In Too Deep*

Bradd Chambers

# Chapter Seventy-Two:

She curses Emmet as she throws herself across the grass towards her car. Starting the engine, she tries again, but her attempts must be in double figures. Still neither of them will answer. What has the bastard done to them?

Ava makes it to the Bull's Horn in just under five minutes. She bursts in the door, scraping her wet hair out of her face as she gets boisterous jeers from the lads at the bar. Ignoring them, she thunders over and slams her fist on the sticky bar top.

"Where's Emmet?"

Macka smirks at her.

"Emmet?"

She groans in frustration.

"Don't be a dick. You know full well who I'm talking about."

Macka sniggers, before lifting the top of the bar and nodding his head towards the back door. She follows him on in, despite the feet stomping and cheers from the locals, out into a tiny corridor with barrels of booze. Macka unlocks the rickety back door and stands back to let her through.

She finds herself in a thin alleyway overtaken with huge dumpsters full of broken glass. The dimmed street light flickers an eerie light through the huge metal gate. Why is she here? She's about to ask Macka when he snaps the door behind her. The hairs stand up on the back of her neck as she shivers. Is she trapped? Is there a way out? She turns around to see if there's any means of escape to come face to hood with a lonely figure. Just about making out a snarled expression and bad breath. She goes to scream but a cloth is pushed against her face and an arm around her head. She's pulled down to knee height and receives one dig to the head. Then... Blackness.

# Chapter Seventy-Three:

Jesus, her head's splitting. She moans as she turns her head to the side. What was she drinking last night? Wine, she guesses. That's the only drink that leaves her feeling like this the next day. She wonders if Mark will be making his traditional hangover fry. A runny egg would help. And some paracetamol. She can't even remember last night. None of it. What the hell is that digging into her leg? She twists her arm from underneath her and goes to investigate. She's shocked to feel a hard spring sticking out of her mattress. For fuck sake, she only got this recently.

She chances her arm with the light of the room, opening one eye delicately. Darkness. Opening both. Still... Darkness. That's when she realises. She isn't in her bed. She isn't at home. Where is she? She goes to lift her head and it bounces off something solid, jolting her head back down again. As if the throbbing in her head couldn't get any worse. She screws up her eyes against the pain. White light. Her hands snap to her face, pushing her fingers into her eyes to distract herself.

When the majority of it has subsided, she opens her eyes again. She feels around for some familiarity, but she's so confined, at first, she thinks she's in a coffin. She fights down panic. Buried alive. Her biggest fear. But no, it's too tight, too circular. And it's too soft beneath her. She feels around some more, before her hand rests on what she thought was the broken spring. Turns out it's something sticking out of the carpet-like ground. She massages it frantically. It feels like... A jack. A car jack. That's it! She's in a boot. She has to be. Why is she in the boot of a car?

Then, it all comes crashing back to her. Her mum. Emmet. The Bull's Horn. She takes a sharp intake of breath, fear rising. Where is she? What is he going to do with her? And what has he done to her mum? To Robyn? She begins to scream for help, hammering her hands on the roof above her. But she quickly becomes exhausted, her efforts futile. She knows it. If he's taken her somewhere in the boot of his car, she'll hardly be sitting in the middle of Shipquay Street. No, she'll be out somewhere where no one will hear her. Be able to help her. She thinks of her phone sitting on the passenger seat of her car and curses herself for her stupidity. Out here, wherever she is. And with no means of escape... She's a sitting duck.

# Chapter Seventy-Four:

It's been hours since she gave up trying. Desperately kicking and battering everything around her in an attempt to free herself. Her body aches, her knuckles cut and bruising. Her feet not much better. She drifts in and out of fitful sleep, her body still yearning it for recovery, her adrenaline coming in short bursts. Claustrophobia dispersing as fast as it came.

She tries and fails to calculate a plan. The sharpest thing in here is the jack, and she hasn't the energy, nor the room, to pull up the boot cover to get to it. She's too weak to fight him off right now. She's gone so long without food the mere thought of her favourite dish makes her gag. Nothing comes up. Her throat feels blistered. Yearning for some liquid. She thinks about those documentaries and films she's watched where people drink their own urine to survive. There would be no form of container to collect it, and she can't bring herself to even attempt it. Her adult brain still telling her that she isn't on a toilet. Not that she needs to go anyway. She sucked the last strands of moisture from her shampoo-tasting hair hours ago.

What's made worse is what started just over an hour ago now... It must be. She can only guess. She felt like someone was attacking the car. Loud bursts that made her jump. She wondered if she was in a breaker's yard. In a machine that was going to crush her at any minute. But after she stopped flinching and realised that nothing was coming down on her, she guessed it was rain. She listens to it now, thundering down on top of her. Wishing there was a crack in the boot where she could steal some drips of water. Her cheeks sticking together inside her mouth and lips cracked. She doesn't even think she'll be able to scream now even if she did hear someone coming to help.

As she thinks this, she's startled as the car bursts to life. She gets battered about the boot as the vehicle starts its journey. What's happening? Where is he taking her? She tries to muster all her energy for a fight as she feels the rough terrain under her smooth out and the car building speed.

*In Too Deep*

Bradd Chambers

\*\*\*\*

He hiccups as he raises his hands to Jordy, his request for another whiskey. He usually doesn't drink whiskey. It sends him over the edge of drunk. He's pissed Ava's bed on occasion. And he blacks out. Ava telling him things the next day that he's said and done that doesn't sound anything like him, and he can't piece the puzzle of the night before back together no matter how much time passes. Mark thanks Jordy as he swigs another drink of the harsh liquid. His throat burning, not yet accustom to the drink he's been off for so long.

He thinks about Ava. How he wouldn't be drinking this if they hadn't broken up. Just to spite her without her knowledge, he thinks. Stupid really. Juvenile. Nothing like him. What is he without her? The past few days he knows he's been a mess. Spitting requests at people and returning one-word answers. Finding the leak in the roof today didn't help his mood. He called his friend Steven, who isn't sure whether the damage has always been there, or whether the torrential rain had caused it. Either way, it needs fixed. Which requires money and man power. Pushing the opening of his business back a few more days, or maybe weeks.

No one brave enough to climb onto the roof to investigate in the storm, he had bitterly sent them home before driving over to the Icon.

Now, here he sits. Contemplating what he's going to do. He doesn't want anyone else. He just wants Ava. He really thought that he was going to spend the rest of his life with her, as cliché as that sounds. When he saw her at the party, he just knew instantly. An initial attraction. Even when he found out she was still only 17, he knew it was just a speed bump. Then, everything that happened within her family... It just brought them closer together. He half tried to talk it out with Paul, who just kept bringing it back to her age.

"She was too young to start going steady," he'd said last night over the phone. "She's obviously looking back on it now and wondering where her wild years went, mate. You remember being that age, don't you?"

Mark had agreed. He had went to university in Birmingham and was constantly out partying and womanizing. But now as he thinks back on it... Ava was different. *Is* different. He hadn't a care in the world except for his next looming essay. She had suffered, making her more mature. She didn't care about parties and socialising. It was him who had to drag her to events to help with her business. And it was just weeks ago that she was thinking he was going to ask her to move in with him.

Maybe that's what started her off? Thinking things weren't going anywhere, and so she started seeing that lad. But no... That's not right. That was the night with the red shoes. Signed from *'M.'* Did she lie about the note too? After all, his name doesn't start with an *'M,'* doesn't it not? What was his name again? Cathal, or something? He pictures him in his mind, his grasp tightening on the whiskey glass. What an asshole. Does he know about Mark? Do they laugh about him? Oh, he's working tonight so they can get together. Have sex in the bed he sleeps in every few nights. He doesn't want to even humour the idea.

A tap on his shoulder breaks his thoughts.

"Mark, isn't it?"

Mark's mouth falls open. It's him. Cathal. What is he doing here? He's got some balls, he'll give him that. Mark turns back towards the bar, reigning in his temper.

"Look, my name's Cathal."

Little known fact, Mark thinks.

"I'm a friend of Ava's."

Friend? Don't make me laugh, he almost says out loud.

"Look... I think we've got off on the wrong foot."

Mark can't help himself. He stands up, squaring up to him. Cathal's just over five foot with weedy arms and thick glasses. Mark must look like a giant towering over him.

"Are you fuckin' serious, lad?" Mark laughs in his face. "Fuck off, now."

"Look, it's not what you think."

"I don't want to hear it, man. So get out now. My family has done business with the manager here. I could get you thrown out in a heartbeat. But I'm giving you one more chance to save yourself the embarrassment. Something you never done for me, but hey... Maybe I'm the nice guy after all. No matter what Ava told y-"

"Mark, I'm gay!"

Cathal shouts the last word, making several people at neighbouring tables turn their heads. Mark just stares at him, trying to detect a hint of a lie. But he stands there proud. Shoulders back. Not so much as a tremor in his voice.

"You're... You're gay?"

*In Too Deep*

Bradd Chambers

# Chapter Seventy-Five:

Despite it being night time outside, the change from the darkness still shocks her as he opens the boot. She strains her eyes against the newfound light. The rain thunders down on top of her. She catches a few drops on her tongue and the rest is shrouded over her. Dampening her clothes within seconds. It's as if she's experienced a new lease of life. The air and the rain bring out all her conserved energy that she didn't know she had. Her elbows help her bolt upright, ready to jump out of the boot.

But before she has a chance, in one swift movement he has a knife pushed against her neck, starting to break skin. She turns to him in shock. He's still got the hood up, but his piercing eyes can't hide in the shadows.

"Get out slowly and get into the car."

She struggles out, both from fear and slipping with the wet, before pulling open the back door to the car and sliding in. She's shocked to see him joining her, slamming the door and cutting off the sound of the storm and the world outside.

"I take it you and your ma have had a nice catch up and you know who I am?"

Ava's eye flickers with an idea.

"Look, you've got the wrong person. My ma is dead. She killed herself years and years-"

Without warning, he grabs the back of her head and slams it off the headrest in front of her. So hard she hears a crack and the blood splatters down her front, making her even damper.

"Don't fuckin' lie to me, girly. I know exactly who ye are. If your ma wasn't dead, ye wouldn't have rushed over to the Bull's Horn, now would ye? Ye would've taken me up as a prank caller or something. Now, where's my money?"

Ava opens her eyes and splutters through the blood. Only now does she realise that she's in her own car. She takes a side glance to the front passenger seat, but can't find her phone. Maybe it's on the floor? Or slid down the side? If she can get him to leave, she could find it and call for help. She has no idea where she is, but she doesn't dare check her surroundings while that knife is millimetres from opening a wound in her neck.

"What money?"

She screams as he goes to grab her again. This time grabbing the back of her head and pulling her closer to him, until they're inches from each other's faces. His breath stinks of ale and his nose looks like it's been broken more than once.

"You're not stupid, girly. And neither am I. We know exactly what's happening here, so unless ye want me to start taking fingers off, I'd play along nicely. Ye hear me?"

She sobs a while longer before nodding. He shoves her away with such force she bangs her already throbbing head off the window. Moaning and reaching around to massage it, she decides to have a quick glance out of the front window whilst her neck is free. It's too dark and the rain is coming down in sheets. She has no idea where she is. She could be anywhere.

"Now, where is my money?"

"It's in the charity's bank account."

"And how did ye get it?"

She goes quiet. She doesn't want to get her mum in anymore trouble. She just stares at him with pleading eyes. Trying to think of a way out.

"Your ma gave ye it, didn't she?"

"What have you done with her?"

"Didn't she?"

The knife is back at her throat again. One fist clenched around her front, pulling her torso closer to him. She continues to cry before nodding sullenly.

"Which card is it?"

He lets go of her jacket and reaches into the front driver's seat, bringing back her handbag she'd left in the car. She thinks against pretending that she doesn't have the card, deciding cooperation is going to be the only way to keep her mother alive. She brings out the card from her purse and everything is snatched out of her shaking hands.

"Pin?"

She gulps.

"Pin?" Emmet spits, more aggressively now.

"0215."

"The month and year your ma left you. How

fitting," he chuckles darkly, before taking the knife from her throat and stepping out of the car.

Slamming the door behind him and locking her in straight away, she immediately dives across the car and starts tearing around the passenger seat. Trying everything short of ripping holes in the fabric. Where is her phone? Her heart beats in her throat as she ignores the groans of her delicate fingers as they snag on bits of chair as she digs around underneath and either side.

A knock at the window makes her jump. Pushing her hair out of her face, she sees Emmet standing with his face pressed against the window, a smirk engulfing his features. In his free hand, he shakes something at her. Something she now realises, upon closer inspection, is her phone.

# Chapter Seventy-Six:

He returns about a half hour later with a bundle of money. Clutching it in his greedy hands, he pockets it once he sees she's noticed. There's no way he could've taken everything in that account out of an ATM. There are limits.

"Just making sure ye gave me the right pin, girly."

It's like he read her mind.

"I'll go about different ones and fish out the rest once I'm done with ye."

Panic rises. Done with her?

"Now, unlock this phone."

He brandishes her phone in front of her eyes.

"The pin ye gave me doesn't work on the passcode. So either tell me or put your finger against it. Whatever stupid burglar-proof shit they have on 'em these days."

Doing as she's told, Ava presses her thumb against the home button, her phone lighting up in front of her. She notices all the missed calls and messages. How long had she been locked in that boot?

"Now, what's that big hunky boyfriend of yours called, eh?"

Her heart stops. What is he going to do?

"Why?" she manages, her voice a squeak, barely audible against the rage of the wind and rain outside.

"Because I'm sure ye don't want me to find him and put him through a similar situation, now do ye?"

Ava bites her lip.

"Mark," she sniffs.

"Mark..." He flicks through her phone, looking up to make sure she's still how he left her every few seconds. "Here he is."

He begins typing, although slow with the thumb of his left hand, his right still wrapped around the knife pressed against her throat. Several moments later, she hears the signature *'beep'* that indicates a sent message, before he turns the machine off and pockets it.

"That ought to do it, now... With you," he smirks again.

She begins to shake uncontrollably, her teeth clattering together.

"What have you done with my mum and Robyn?"

The knife probes deeper into her, making her gasp.

"Your ma and your aunt are somewhere safe. Don't ye worry. I have 'em right where I want 'em," he twists the knife again, she feels a bead of blood slither its way down into her chest. "But you... On the other hand. Are a wee trouble maker. Ye were back then... And ye are now. So, how can we get rid of ye?"

His eyes shine.

"I can see the papers now. *'Tragic suicidal daughter follows in her mother's footsteps.'*"

Ava begins to blubber. No!

"Has a nice ring to it, don't ye think? A nice close on the chapter."

"I'll never do it, you'll have to push me."

A bizarre moment to think of her charity. Of her clients. All the people who came to her for help. She'd never let them down like that.

"Well... Ye are. I've noticed cameras are up there now. It's not as simple as it once was. I can't just drive ye up there myself anymore. My face will be everywhere. I'm not about that life. So, you're going to get out of this car and climb that hill," he nods behind him, his rancid teeth glistening in the light above the rear-view mirror. "Come out onto the bridge and jump. And if ye don't? Or ye try to run for help? I'll kill ye myself, only this time I won't be letting your ma and your aunt go. Three in one night would be a record for me."

"You're mad!" Ava screams, ignoring the bite of the knife.

"Maybe," he smirks again. "Now I know ye, Ava. You're a smart, caring girly. Ye don't want your ma to end up like my exes."

"Your exes?"

She's not sure she wants to know. He brings the knife away, turning the blunt side towards him so the smooth side is against her neck. In a slow motion, he brings it from one side to the other, one eyebrow raised. She starts crying again, the cold metal exposing her vulnerable neck. He's killed before?

"If ye do this, I promise they will be safe. Your ma can come with me like nothing happened. And your aunt? Sure she's away mad. No-one will believe a word she says even if she tries to tout. Will find herself locked up in Gransha as a worst-case scenario. So, girly. Are ye going to listen to every single word I say?"

Hesitantly, Ava nods, blinded by tears and the knowledge that she has no other choice.

*In Too Deep*

\*\*\*\*

Mark and Cathal laugh as they thank Jordy for the next round of pints.

"I can't believe all this time she's been telling the truth."

Cathal nods as he sips the head of his beer.

"Of course. Nothing ever happened, nor was it going to."

"In that case," Mark pulls a face. "Who was sending her all those presents?"

Cathal raises his eyebrow.

"She didn't tell you?"

"No, what?"

"She started getting gifts to her door. Started off with shoes. Then flowers. She started to get really freaked out. Said she believed it was Darrell Boyle, the politician. That he was threatening her or blackmailing her. I don't know... It's been a hard few weeks."

Cathal nods again.

"She never told me any of this, Mark. It seems like she's in a really dark place right now."

Mark shrugs.

"I know... And I haven't exactly been there for her," he looks up from his pint towards Cathal. "She needed a friend... Thanks for being there."

Cathal beams before reaching his hand out for Mark to shake for the fourth or fifth time. It's cut short as Mark pulls his phone out from his back pocket after his message tone sounds. His eyes widen as he looks back at Cathal, swivelling the phone around so he can read the text.

*'cant do this anymre, mark. i lvoe you but. ur betr of wifot me. this is gdbye.'*

# Chapter Seventy-Seven:

Now, here she is. On top of the Foyle Bridge. Looking down into the swollen river, the water breaking its banks out onto the surrounding land, close to where Emmet parked. She had found it hard meandering her way up the hill in the dark and wind, but eventually made it. Knowing full well that Emmet's eyes were glaring into her back.

She stands at the railings, one foot on the bottom, ready to climb over. Shaking furiously. Shocked that she's doing this. She never thought she'd know how it felt to look down there and know that it's the last sight she'll see. Thinking it was the last thing her mother ever seen. Not wanting her clients to feel or see the same. What will people think of her? She can't think of that, she has to focus all her attention on her mother... And the signal.

Emmet had told her what she needed to do. Climb to the top and wait for him to push her car into the water. After all, it *is* crawling with evidence. Her blood and DNA in the back seat and boot. His fingerprints on the wheel. He couldn't risk that, could he? So whenever her car enters the river, so will she. He told her it had rained all day. Several

387

rivers in the city have overflowed, with many floods even in residential areas. The emergency services are all busy. If her car is found in the river, it won't be a surprise. Not tonight. The surprise will come when they find her body...

*If* they find her body, she thinks. Remembering the facts and figures Zoe had told her over the years. Of course she had thought about running away, but she can't be selfish. She has to think of her mum. Of Robyn. Of Mark. Mark... Emmet had told her that he had sent him a message telling him she loved him, but she couldn't do it anymore. The sick bastard even writing her own suicide note for her. But she has that small victory. He'll have that to remember her by.

Lights catch her eye on the cityside and she squints down through the rain. Two beams of light hobble along the grass at a slow pace. Emmet must have the handbrake off and pushing it from behind. It jolts left and right a few more times, before breaking off into the water, which is so dark you can barely make the lights out anymore.

That's the signal.

Taking a deep breath and praying to a God she'd long forgotten about, she begins to hoist herself up. When one leg is over and she's clinging onto the barriers, she remembers Robyn's story. Her made-up story, she now recollects. Of how Robyn found Ava's mum in this exact position.

She closes her eyes and thinks of them both. And of Mark. She tries several times to relax her body, so she can just slide off, but she can't bring herself to do it. She decides she'll bring her other leg round and just jump.

But just as she's swinging the leg around, she sees a car oncoming from the Waterside. She gasps. Should she jump now? Get it over and done with? Will they stop? Will they try and talk her down? Can she try and ask them for help? So many thoughts run through her mind before her brain recognises the car. It's Mark. And right there, in his front seat, is her mother. Her tense body relaxes just as another strong wind comes. She fights to hold on but ends up slipping from the railings.

Bradd Chambers

\*\*\*\*

I scream, pushing the car door open and run over to the railings. My baby girl. No, this can't be happening. This can't be how it ends. When I reach the side of the bridge, I let out a huge sigh of relief, before calling the rest over. She's still clinging on with one hand.

"It's alright, Ave. It's alright," I bellow down to her.

She gazes up at me with huge scared eyes, reminding me of when she was just a child. Making me say something I thought I'd never say again.

"Mummy's here. Mummy's here."

With the help of Mark and his friend, we battle the elements and struggle to bring her over the railings, each of us taking turns to embrace her once she's back on our side. Robyn joining when she hobbles over. She's soaking and has blood all over herself. What has she done? She hasn't answered any of our messages since last night. I blame myself. This was all too much for her. It got the better of her.

Only when she's safely in the backseat of Mark's car does she indulge us on what's been happening.

"You're okay. You guys are okay. How did you escape?"

Robyn and I share concerned looks.

"Escape?"

"Emmet told me he'd captured you both. He texted me telling me to meet him in a bar if I wanted you guys to live. I got there and he knocked me out. I've been in my boot for... I don't even know how long."

She stares at us desperately,

"When was I at yours?" she glances at Mark's dashboard, reading the time.

"Erm... You left at like five o'clock yesterday," Robyn eyes her.

"Fuck!" Ava screams, kicking the chair in front of her. "That bastard had me locked in the boot for nearly 24 hours."

When she opens her eyes and begins to calm down, she stares at Mark's friend. As if she's just registering his presence.

"Cathal, what are you doing here?"

Cathal and Mark now look at one another.

"We were out for a pint," Mark smiles.

"What?" Ava burrows her brow, before shaking her head.

She must be delusional. Or has decided there's more pressing matters.

"Why are you all here? How did you find me?"

"Well," Mark grabs her hand. "When you sent that text, Cathal and I were in the Icon. We tried ringing you, but your phone went straight to voicemail. So I tried Robyn. She told me to come pick her and her friend up," he nods towards me. "And that's when we came onto the bridge. It was our first choice. Thank God we found you, what were you thinking?"

"I wasn't thinking. I wasn't doing it for me, Mark. You all have to believe me. He told me he wanted rid of me. That I was a troublemaker, apparently. He wanted me to kill myself so he could run off with you," she nods towards me. "And if Robyn tried to tell anyone that no-one would believe her 'cause she's mad. Took the charity money and everything. He's down there now. On the banking. He pushed my car into the water to get rid of the evidence and was waiting for me to jump."

I shake my head furiously, a blinding rage coming over me. The boys look about them confused but both myself and Robyn are flared with raw emotion. I can't believe it. And I don't think twice. Despite their calls of protest and reluctance, I'm out of the car and running for the banking. Down to Emmet, but I don't care. He can do whatever he wants to me but how dare he come for my daughter.

Bradd Chambers

# Chapter Seventy-Eight:

The rain has finally petered out by the time the remaining four get down to the bank. The normal walkway has flooded, so they squish around on the sodden grass, too afraid to shout Fiona's name. Would he have left once he saw what was happening on the bridge? Ava isn't so sure. What if he waited for her? Ambushed her? Took her God knows where? They could be halfway to their old life in Belfast, or new life somewhere else, by now.

Ava finds her mother down near where her car had been parked. They can see the tyre tracks from where the car was pushed into the river.

"Fee," Robyn shouts carry across the wind.

She turns towards them and waves. They're almost upon her when a shadow comes from behind the bushes, grabbing her and forcing a familiar looking knife to her neck. They all gasp. It's him.

"Turn around and go back to where ye came from and no-one gets hurt," comes the voice from behind the hood.

The four subconsciously make a semi-circle around him. There's no escape. He's trapped. If he goes any further back, he'll enter the water.

"I mean it. I've killed before. I have no problem just slicing her throat and throwing her into the river. Now get back, I say. I want ye al-"

"Dad?"

Ava's head snaps to her left. Towards Cathal. Emmet stops what he's saying, his head turned towards Cathal. Spluttering a few words, before recollecting his thoughts.

"Everyone move back and away from me if ye want her to live. Let us go in peace. We're in love. We'll be on our way an-"

"Dad, let her go."

He groans before pulling back his hood.

"Get out of the way, Cath."

"Dad, what the fuck are you doing?"

"I'm asking ye all to leave me alone. Me and her had a great life away from ye all, and we will again. So move now, or you'll all be sorry."

"He's your dad?" Mark looks astounded.

Cathal and Ava meet eyes before he nods. Ava stares at Emmet, free from a hood and out in the moonlight. Although years and years older, there's no denying that that's the same guy from the picture sitting in Cathal's house. How had she not noticed? Had Cathal known all this time? She doubts so, judging by the look on Emmet's face. He looks... Embarrassed.

"You've killed before..."

"Awk, Cathal don't play soft. Ye really think your ma and Orla's ma just walked out on me? On *me,* like? I'm the fuckin' best thing happened 'em. Naw, hardly. They're both buried beneath that new shed I built out the back."

Ava gasps, shaking her head. What a monster. She hears vomit hitting the ground from her left, but she doesn't dare take her eyes off the man. Off the knife. Too afraid of what he'll do to her mum.

"Now, man. I think you need to leave that lady alone," Mark begins to step forward, arms held up so Emmet can see that he's unarmed.

"Stand back ye cunt," Emmet struggles back, constantly looking behind him.

The water slowly creeping ever closer.

"What you've said tonight is fine, mate. Just go on. We won't say a thing. Take the money. How much money is that, now? You could get far with that. Never have to be found. Just go, but please leave the lady behind."

Mark's always been like this. Thinks he can resolve any situation. Even though he has absolutely no idea what's going on. Emmet's feet must be wet now, you can hear them squelching underneath the grass. He must be inches from the water's edge. His eyes focused on Mark, mere feet away from him.

"Stand back, boy. I won't tell ye again. You think I won't kill her 'cause I love her?" he chuckles darkly. "It's never stopped me before."

"Mate, just-"

It all happens so fast. Mark takes a step forward and Emmet takes a jab at him, but when he recoils, he loses his balance and falls into the river, dragging Fiona in along with him.

"Mum!" Ava screams.

Without hesitation, Mark dives in after them.

"No, Mark. Don't!"

But it's too late. He's already nowhere to be seen. Ava, Robyn and Cathal stand at the side of the river watching for any signs of life. Straining their eyes against the darkness and their ears against the howling of the wind. It's almost impossible. Cathal even brings out his phone and turns on his torch app, but the weak light doesn't even break the surface of the water closest to them, never mind further out.

"There," Cathal shouts a few moments later, pointing to a part about thirty metres downstream, rushing along the banks, shortly followed by the ladies.

Moments later, they see two figures fighting with the current, bobbing in and out of the water. Are they fighting with the current or with each other? Or both? No, it looks like one is clinging to the other for support. Attempting to climb onto the other for safety. But it's too dark and they're too far away for them to see properly. Ava gets an idea.

"Rob, do you still have Zoe's number?"

Robyn nods, handing over her phone.

"Hiya, Robyn. Long time n-"

"Zoe, it's me. Ava. There are three people in the river. Quick, please, hurry. We're just under the new bridge. One of them is Mark."

She hangs up then, just as she sees shadows moving close to shore. The water's calmer here. Just shy of the fast flow downstream. Cathal is able to jump in to knee height and, moments later, retrieve one of the figures fighting with the current.

"Oh, thank God. Mum!"

Ava jumps in and meets them halfway, helping bring her mother to shore. She coughs and splutters, before lying on the ground gasping for air.

"Mum, are you okay?"

Fiona nods, still coughing, looking up at her daughter.

"I can't lose you again. Mum."

"You won't, love."

Ava wipes the tears from her eyes. Relief leaving her as she examines the water, searching for Mark.

"Where's Mark?" Fiona's chest still sounds like it's filled with water as Robyn wraps her in her old shawl.

"I don't know, Mum."

"He made me grab onto him. He swam me out of the current. I thought he was right behind me."

Ava shakes her head. That asshole. He'd gone back to try and save Emmet. He always plays the hero card, even now when it can get him fucking killed.

# Chapter Seventy-Nine:

The rescue boats come and go, but still there's no sign of the men. The foursome sit in the ambulance with giant sheets that look like tinfoil wrapped around them. After Fiona had been looked over by a professional, they were left alone with their mugs of too-sweet tea. Ava had fought with them, saying she wanted to go look. To help. But they told her it was ridiculous. Everywhere was flooded. They didn't even know what shape the banks were in. One slip could result in her falling in too. It takes all her energy to keep her bum on the seat in the ambulance, her legs jiggling with apprehension.

"This is all my fault," Fiona gazes out onto the river. "All my fault."

"Don't say that, Fee."

"But it is, Robyn. I was the one brought this monster into our lives. I was the one that went with him instead of taking my chances with that stupid gang. I messed everything up. I always have. Always bloody will."

Ava hugs her mum as tight as physically possible with the giant sheets separating their embrace.

"Alright, Mrs Friel. How are you doing?"

They all look up to see an older looking volunteer shuffling up the bank towards them.

"Erm... Grand, Frank. And yourself?"

"What's brought you all here tonight, then? It isn't the boys in the water, is it?"

They all nod.

"Jesus. Nasty business that. Your family have a rough time of it, don't they? First your sister, then your husband. Who's this now?"

Ava and Fiona's heads snap towards Robyn, their mouths gaping wide.

"Ah... A friend of the family tonight now, Frank."

"God love yees, I hope we find them safe and well," he nods towards them before trudging back up towards the road.

An awkward silence befalls the back of the ambulance. That is, before Ava and Fiona's shouts burst out at once.

"*'Your husband?'*"

"Uncle Damien?"

"What the hell does he mean *'your husband?'*"

"You told me Uncle Damien was up in Letterkenny doing some work."

"What's going on, Robyn?"

They both fall silent, staring at her. Robyn smiles sweetly towards Cathal, who takes a while to get the hint, before coughing and making his way back up towards the road.

"Tell us, Robyn. Now!"

Robyn flinches at the force of her sister's order.

"Look... Damien and I... We went through a rough patch."

"A rough patch?" Ava laughs. "You were constantly at each other's throats. That isn't a rough patch, Rob."

"Aye I know, I know. Right... Well... I'm sorry to bring it up, and don't take any blame please, Fee. But once you left... I found it so hard to cope with your secret. I took to drink and prescription drugs. My head was fried. A complete mess. Then, when Ava left... I stopped cleaning the house and cooking dinner. There were times he would come home and he'd find me in the exact position that he left me in. Just gazing out the window. It took its toll.

"Then... One day... He had to go to Belfast for some conference. And he came back and he just... Wasn't the same. I asked him what was wrong and he just ignored me. He left and came back in the early hours of the morning completely steaming. I've never seen him that drunk, and you remember your Uncle Damien. He couldn't drink for shite. He started arguing with me, saying that I was a horrible person. I'd had a few myself, so didn't even attempt to fight back... Then he told me."

The pair know what's coming before she says it. Robyn stares into her sister's eyes, guilt etched over her face.

"He saw you. Up in Belfast. Must've been on one of your outings. He'd come straight home, not even bothering with the second half of his conference. He asked me if it was true. Asked if I knew. I hesitated, and that was enough confirmation for him. He burst into tears and slammed the front door in my face.

"I never heard from him again. A few weeks later, the police were at my door. Said they'd found a body in the river. The dental records matched his. I told them not to release his name. I was the only family he had. I couldn't do it to you, Ave. I couldn't have someone else... Disappear from your life."

Ava shakes her head at her aunt. Irony not wasted on her that Damien *had* disappeared, even before now. She can't believe what she's hearing. All this time and she'd kept everything inside. No wonder her mind wasn't what it used to be.

"I need to be on my own."

"Ave, wait."

She ignores both of the women's protests and batters downhill, towards the river. A few yards short from the water, she collapses onto the soaking grass and bursts into tears. She lies there and cries. Cries for her mum. Cries for Mark. Cries for Robyn. Cries for Uncle Damien. Cries for herself and what she'd gone through. Not only the past three years, but the weeks and days leading up to tonight.

When the tears stop coming, she sits up and lets herself sink into the ground, looking out onto the lights currently searching the river for her boyfriend and the murderer who had almost made her commit suicide.

# Chapter Eighty:

They lie on Ava's sofa and watch the TV. Her mother and her. It feels weird, having her in this house. A house that was bare of memories of her. The news is on. They watch the carnage that was last night. But not their carnage. No, Derry's carnage. Millions of pounds of damage for the city. Bridges collapsed. Homes destroyed. Cars washed away.

Then, when the locals are finished being interviewed, the news reporter stands at the side of the Foyle Bridge, telling them that two bodies *'accidentally'* entered the river last night. That makes Ava's blood boil. People will think they were drunk. That they fell in. Mark should be made out to be a hero. He jumped in and saved her mother, despite not even knowing who she was, and went back to save a psychopath who was going to kill him mere moments before. He should be celebrated, not brushed off as a hopeless case.

They'd made it home after midnight last night. The roads were so bad with the floods the ambulance had to go a special way. They were surprised Robyn's house wasn't affected, being so close to the water's edge. Luckily, everything was untouched. They'd barely said goodbye to her as she left them. They'll ring her later today and see how she's got on. If all of this has taught them one thing, it's that you don't know what someone else is thinking, no matter how strong their front. They can't stay angry at her forever, she has no one else.

A knock at the door makes them jump. Ava stands, smoothing her top before they make their way to the front door. There stand two police officers. And by the look on their faces, they aren't here to give good news.

"Oh, no," Ava doubles over, grief flooding through her.

Her mother helps the female officer pick her up off the wooden floor in the hallway and rest her on the sofa. They say that two bodies were found. They believe they're a match for Mark and Emmet. They didn't make it. She doesn't take any of it in. It's as if they're talking to someone else. About someone else. Then, as if a TV on mute, she can't hear them at all. There's a ringing in her ears and she just stares at the carpet.

Her mother does a lot of talking beside her, but she doesn't hear what she says. Maybe she's explaining herself? Revealing who she really is? Will she go to prison? Be made to make statements and stand up in court? She's not sure.

She's aware of them moving around her, but she just focuses on the ground. Thinking of all the times she spent with Mark in this very room. How they'd had their whole lives in front of them. But now? She had taken all that away from him.

Bradd Chambers

\* \* \* \*

Cathal closes the front door after the police leave. They didn't know his dad had even been missing. He'd been worried that they would be taking him up for fraud. Luckily, they hadn't made the link… Yet. He hopes they won't. To them, his dad was a delinquent that had found himself in the wrong place at the wrong time.

He's sure that Ava and her mother will be telling the police their side of the story. But for all they know, his dad still could've been collecting his brew. He knows Jimmy, his dad's mate in the dole office, won't tell the police squat. Would rather spit on them. He's safe.

That's when he becomes aware that he should feel much more than fear that he might have been being imprisoned. He should be upset. Crying. Angry. Aren't those the stages of grief? Cathal isn't sure. His dad was never there for him, and he'd been absent for so long that it's weird to actually know that he's dead. He'd never made much of an impact on his life.

Now, Ava. Ava had. He thinks on the times to come. The times she'll invite him for drinks and movie nights to talk about their similar situations.

Playback last night and the different scenarios that could've happened. Share their grief. An event like this will glue them together for a long time, if not for life. That's plenty of time to get to know one another properly. Perhaps be more than friends? Indulge their darkest secrets to one another until she knows him inside out? But there's always something that he'll keep from her. That he'll keep from everyone. Keep in the dark that last night, when Fiona and Mark were attempting to struggle out of the water, Fiona near collapsing, he'd done something sick. Something that makes him believe he is his father's son.

"Here, take her," Mark had coughed, unknowingly throwing his girlfriend's mother towards safety, whilst Cathal had taken all of Fiona's weight off him, resting her in the shallow water.

Mark continued to fight against the current, splashing about and constantly getting pushed downstream. He had reached a hand out for Cathal to take. Cathal reluctantly took it, before getting an idea. Pulling him from the tide, Mark's body relaxed. Gasping for gulps of air. With one swift movement, pretending like he was turning around to check on Fiona, who was still dipping in and out of consciousness beside him, he'd turned around so aggressively, bumping all his weight onto Mark, who lost all balance, scrabbled around for something to grab onto, before dropping once again into the current.

And just like that, Mark was gone, snapped up by the undertow. Cathal saw his face. His eyes.

Shock. Betrayal. Fear. That is, until the black water swallowed him up... And upon hearing the police's reports this morning, it looks like it has finished with him, and has finally spat him back out again.

# A Note From The Author:

Although the majority of this book has been spurted out from my imagination, there's still the underlying theme that will hit home with the people of Derry, and those around the world. Suicide and depression *are* stigmas, and the battles that Ava is facing in this novel are being faced in real life by people all over the world, especially in Derry. The Foyle Bridge is notorious for bringing the end to so many people's lives. Young or old. Man or woman. Catholic or Protestant. It doesn't care what victim is next.

We as a city need to stand together to help fight this deadly killer. Although not mentioned in the book, there are around 40 different organisations in Derry City targeting mental health, including Me 4 Mental and Aware NI to name a few. These people are doing what Ava is doing. They want people to talk about their problems. I believe no problem is too big or too small that risks you losing your life over. And I can say that hand on heart as someone who has also battled with mental health throughout my life.

The Foyle Search and Rescue are also mentioned in the book and are a real organisation who work tirelessly around the clock to make the water a safer place. I can't begin to imagine the sights they've seen and news they've had to give, but still they continue what they're doing on a voluntary basis to help the people of this city.

If you've enjoyed this book or have been bitten by the real-life problems and issues that the characters deal with, I would please urge you to donate to these causes. They need all the support they can get. Donations can be taken on their respective websites. Thank you.

*In Too Deep*

Bradd Chambers

# About The Author:

Bradd Chambers grew up on the outskirts of Derry~Londonderry in Northern Ireland. From a young age, he started reading and writing stories. He exceeded in English at school, and went on to obtain an NCTJ Diploma in Journalism at his local college, before graduating with a 2:1 in the same subject from Liverpool John Moores University. He has studied Creative Writing for years at colleges around the UK.

He currently writes for several online magazines. Bradd's debut novel *'Someone Else's Life'* was released in June 2017, with the prequel novella, *'Our Jilly,'* following in November of the same year. Bradd is currently working on several stand-alones, with another based in his hometown of Derry also in the pipeline.

*"Thank you so much for taking the time to read my stories and helping to make my dream of becoming an author possible. If you enjoyed* 'Our Jilly,' *or any other of my books, please don't forget to spread the word through word of mouth and/or social media. Also, a review on Amazon or Goodreads goes an awful long way, especially for Indie authors like myself who a lot of people haven't heard of."*

Bradd Chambers

Printed in Poland
by Amazon Fulfillment
Poland Sp. z o.o., Wrocław